W IS

JIMMY?

BY

J. N. STEPHENSON

ISBN-13: 978-1-9993656-9-1

DEDICATION

*I dedicate this book to my fantastic mum and all others who
are living and caring for someone with dementia.
My mum is so caring and always has supported me in my
life and the writing of my books.*

To all my characters some of which are real people
- you know who you are, I thank you all.

CONTENTS

CHAPTER 1

FREE AS A BIRD

I woke to the sound of the buzzer and as I opened my eyes I smiled; this was the day I walked out of this hell hole.

I threw my legs over the edge of my bunk and dropped to the floor.

"Morning, you lucky man. You're a free man today, Craig."

I turned to see Bobby lying in his bed. Bobby was in for murder; he was 42 years old and had 6 years still to do on his sentence. He was of heavy, muscly build, covered in tattoos and with no hair he looked menacing, but during the 2 years I had spent as his cellmate we got on well together and never had any trouble.

"Alright, mate. Yep, I can't wait till I get out and breathe some clean air."

I walked towards the toilet and had a piss. As I flushed the chain and lifted my toothbrush Bobby got out of bed and plunked his arse on the toilet.

"Nothing like an early morning shit to wake you up, Craig."

"That's one thing I won't miss, the smell of you in the mornings."

Bobby laughed as he squeezed one out and yep, he stunk the cell out. I even heard the guys in the next cell shout in, "Fir fuck's sake, Bobby, you are stinking."

Bobby just laughed and finished off his shit and with no dignity he wiped his arse and pulled his boxers up.

The stench of him was so bad you could actually taste it in the air so with a couple of swirls of water round my mouth, I spat it out and then cupped a handful of the cold water and threw it around my face. I dried my hands and face with the old blue towel that hung beside the sink, I put some deodorant on – which sort of masked the smell of Bobby – and then got dressed.

Instead of the grey bottoms and white t-shirt that were prison issue, I had been given back my clothes that I had worn the day I was found guilty of ABH and robbery. I had been given a sentence of 30 months with a chance of early release on probation after 24.

I put my socks on, then my denim jeans and the fusty-smelling brown jumper that had seen better days, and with my worn-down trainers I was ready to go; another spray of deodorant and I was set.

As the buzzer sounded for breakfast and the steel door unlocked, both Bobby and I walked out of our cell and onto the landing where we followed the rest of the inmates to the dinner hall.

I got some strange looks from some of the guys and a few smart comments as well but I just laughed them off and held my head up as I knew I would never see them again.

It was the usual crap for breakfast — a bowl of tasteless porridge and then scrambled eggs that ran off your plate with a couple of slices of cremated bacon and 2 rounds of burnt toast, but to be honest I enjoyed every mouthful 'cause I knew it was the last time I would have to eat it.

It was now 8.45am and I was due for release at 9.30am, so not long to go.

After I finished eating I said my goodbyes to Bobby and a few other inmates that I got on well with and as the buzzer sounded again I was ushered away to another part of the prison, where I had to fill in some paperwork for my release.

It took around 30 minutes and as I was handed a brown envelope containing my personal belongings, the guard shook my hand and said, "I hope everything works out for you, Craig, and we don't see you back in here again."

"So do I, boss, so do I."

"Good luck, Craig," he replied.

I turned and walked towards the exit and as I walked through the door, a free man, the air smelt just that little bit fresher. A couple of deep breaths and as my head cleared I looked up and down the street. I turned and as I walked towards the bus stop I knew where I wanted to go — the place where I was tortured as a child — and I knew what I wanted to do.

CHAPTER 2

CHARITY BEGINS AT HOME

It wasn't long before the number 6 bus came which took me into Liverpool city centre. The journey only took about 20 minutes and with it being a Monday morning the city was alive with shoppers. As I got off the bus I just disappeared into the crowds of faceless people, all wrapped up in their own worlds and troubles.

I was to go to Faulkner Street where I was to meet my probation officer who was going to get me accommodation and a job sorted.

I knew in my head that I would never work again but I needed a couple of days to adjust before I went to the farm where I wanted to confront the evil man who tortured me for years.

I went into the office and gave my name to the girl at reception. As she lifted her head she looked me up and down and asked me, "And who are you here to see?"

"I was told to ask for Veronica, love."

"Don't 'love' me," she replied quite cheekily. "Take a seat and Veronica will see you shortly."

"Thanks." I was quite taken aback by her remarks but she knew exactly why I was here and what I was here for. I was going to have to get used to people making snap judgements about me and just take it on the chin. I turned and sat on one of the many seats that were against the wall opposite her desk.

Ten minutes or so passed and then the girl at the desk lifted her head again. "Veronica will see you now. It's room 3, down the hall."

I stood up. "Thanks very much," I replied in a softly spoken voice and walked down the corridor. I looked at the numbers on each door as I passed and as I got to room 3, I knocked and waited.

I heard a voice from within. "Come in."

I opened the door to a brightly lit room and an oldish woman with grey hair and glasses looking back at me from behind a desk. "Nice to meet you, Craig. Take a seat," she said as she pointed to a seat on my side of the desk. I pulled the chair out and sat down.

"Well, how are you?"

"Still catching my breath," I replied.

"Look, it will take time for you to adjust and we are here to help you do that. Just take a day at a time."

She seemed very understanding but I was under no illusion. I knew they just wanted to keep tabs on me so I wouldn't re-offend.

"I know it will. The last thing I want is to end up inside again so whatever it takes, I'm willing to do."

I learned over the years what to say and when to say it so this was piss easy. I had her in the palm of my hands and she knew it.

"That's the right attitude, Craig. You will make the transition easy with that outlook."

"So, what's first?" I asked.

"Well, we need to get you on the system and get you a roof over your head as well as getting you a job."

"I'm up for that," I replied, knowing good and well I would never start the job.

"Right, we have accommodation for you, it will be right up your street. It's a housing project called Norris Green and it is just a bus ride away from where we have hooked you up with a job."

"That sounds fantastic, and where am I going to be working?" I was actually surprised by what Veronica was telling me. Not too bad for an ex-con on his first day after being released from prison.

"It's a local supermarket. You will be working the night shift stacking shelves, but before you pass any judgement on it, give it a go, you will find that it is quite rewarding getting back into society and not being told what to do and when to do it."

"No, I don't mind what I do, it will just be good getting back to normality." Again, I was letting her hear all the right things.

As she handed me a set of keys and envelope she said, "These are the keys to your new home." And as she handed me the envelope, she said, "Everything you need to know is in here. There is one hundred pounds as well to get you started. You start your new job on Sunday night, your hours are ten at night till six in the morning, but all the details are in here as well."

I took the envelope from her and replied, "I can't believe you have done all this for me. I can't thank you enough."

"Look, Craig, it's nothing personal, this is what I

do. The only thing we require is that you make a meeting here every Monday at 3pm and that we don't get any bad reports from your housing officer and employer."

"I assure you won't get any bad reports. As I told you, I know what is waiting for me if I go back inside and I sure as hell never want to go back there."

"That's great, Craig, then our meeting is over." As she said that she stood up, as did I. She shook my hand and I thanked her again and left.

I went to a side-street café to get a mug of coffee and open the envelope. The coffee wasn't great but it was warm and with the four sugars I put in, it was sweet.

I tore open the envelope and took the money out first and put it in my brown leather wallet. I then lifted the key – it had a tag on it and it read: 22b Norris Green Crescent. I thought to myself, *This must be a flat with it being 'b'.* "Well, it's a roof over my head and I don't need to share the toilet with Bobby," I said softly and I smiled.

The last thing in the envelope was a letter; it was on headed paper which had the Aldi logo on it. I read it to myself. I was to go on Friday morning at 9am for my induction and to get a uniform. I was in two minds. The days leading up to my release, I just wanted to go back to the house and end my nightmares but seeing this letter and set of keys and having a few quid in my pocket, I decided the house could wait. I had another gulp of my coffee and was now intrigued as to what my flat looked like, so I decided to catch the bus to it. I paid for my coffee and left.

It wasn't long before the bus came and I took the short journey to Norris Green estate. I got off at the Crescent and the first door I saw was number 56 so I knew it was only a short walk to get to my flat.

As I walked down the street I looked around the place. It seemed quite a nice area – there weren't many people about and as I counted the doors down I was actually getting a bit excited. I had to check myself and told myself to wise up, *It's only a flat, for goodness' sake,* and there it was, number 22. I stopped and looked at the door. It was a block of four flats; they were white pebble dashed and had white-framed windows. They didn't look half bad. I pushed the door open and went into a hallway; there was a bit of a smell so I propped the door open with a brick that was sitting beside it. As I did that a door opened opposite me and a young lad came walking out. As he lifted his head he looked me square in the eyes. "Hello," I said, waiting for a reply but it didn't come. He just put his head down and shuffled past me. I sort of shook my head but it was the smell of dope that caught my attention. I sighed. I knew what went along with a dope head and what to expect.

I put the key in the door and opened it up; it was dark inside so I felt for a light switch and turned it on. As I closed the door behind me I noticed there wasn't a carpet in the small hallway, just an old bit of vinyl that had a few holes in it. I walked forward and opened up the door that led me into the living room. Again, it was dark so I turned the light on. I walked over to the curtains that hadn't been pulled and opened them up and opened the window to try and air the place out a bit; it wasn't that it smelt but it just needed a bit of fresh air around the place.

I went and turned the light off again and looked around. There wasn't much furniture but what was there was not too bad – a three-piece brown suite, a side table and a TV cabinet, but then again, beggars can't be choosers, I thought.

I then went into the bedroom that was off to the right. It had a single bed, a bedside cabinet and a wardrobe in it. Again, I opened the window to air it out. The kitchen wasn't that big but it had a fridge, a cooker and a microwave that to be honest was done but it worked, so I was happy enough. The last place I looked at was the bathroom and it really did need airing out as it wasn't the cleanest but it had a walk-in shower that just needed a good cleaning, and it worked.

"Well, Craig, this is home for now so you've just got to make the most of it."

I decided to take a walk down the street to see if there was a shop where I could get a few groceries and maybe some products to clean the place up a bit.

Just around the corner there was a row of shops – a convenience store, a wine lodge and a chip shop. I got what I needed from the store and bought a sausage supper from the chip shop. When I got back to my flat I sat and ate my lunch/dinner, as it was nearly 4pm now, and with just having £62 left out of the hundred, I knew I would have to make this money last and not spend it stupidly.

After I finished my chips I got stuck into a bit of cleaning. Before I started I put my shopping away and it was when I opened the fridge door to put the milk and butter in that the smell of sour milk hit me in the face. I actually gagged as it overpowered me. I had smelt some rough things in my day but this was up with the best of them. I held my nose and walked out the back of the flats to find the bins. I was never so glad to get a smell out of my nose.

I spent the next few hours cleaning the whole place and when I finished I felt a bit of self-satisfaction. If I was going to make a go of this place it had to be clean.

I went to bed that night exhausted; it had been a long day but a good day, a good start to my new life.

The next morning I went into town. I needed some clothes as I only had what was on my back and it was a case of charity shops as that's all I could afford. I got a couple of pairs of jeans, a few t-shirts and a coat. I had to go to Primark to get some socks and boxers but all in all for 30 quid I was kitted out but the down side was, I was running out of cash and fast.

With nothing else to do and plenty of time to do it in I decided to save the bus fare and walk home. When I got back I was met by the dope head and again he kept his head down and walked past me. I thought the first time was weird but this guy was bad news; he was off his head and it was only 2.30pm. I propped the door open again just to get rid of the smell and went into my flat.

I put my new clothes away. Well, they weren't new but they were new to me, and I made myself a coffee. I had picked up a wee radio in the charity shop for a quid and that was my company for the next few days until I started work.

When Friday rolled around I was actually glad to go for my induction as I was bored out of my head. I was fed up going for walks just to put the day in so it was a breath of fresh air being shown how to unpack cages of food and household products and getting them stacked properly in rotation, putting the closest selling dates to the front of the shelves. I was chuffed to bits with my uniform – a pair of work trousers, two polo tops, two jumpers and a bodywarmer, but most importantly the work boots that were given to me, as apart from the trainers I had they were the only shoes I had.

My manager was not a bad guy; he was quiet but courteous and explained what was expected of me and that I had to be a team player. That wasn't going to be a problem. I was glad of actually getting to speak with other people, as apart from the girl in the shop and the dope head they would be the only people that I spoke to.

I was due to start my first shift at 10 o'clock on Sunday night so I only had a couple of days to put in.

Over the last few days I started noticing different fellas calling at Dope Head's flat and at different times. I gathered he was doing a bit of dealing as it was the same routine – a car pulls up outside, one fella would get out and come into the dope head's flat. They would never stay too long and away they would go, but it was Saturday night that more than one would call; in fact at one stage there were four or five in his flat and he had his music blasting, which to be honest was OK at first but when it went on until 3 in the morning I was starting to lose the bap as I wanted to go to sleep. I opened my flat door to the waft of dope and there were two guys shooting up on the stairs. They didn't even notice me go over to Dope Head's door and hit it a thump. (*Bang, bang, bang.*) I waited.

No answer so a bit louder I thumped. (*BANG, BANG, BANG.*) This time the door opened and there. out of his head. was Dope Head. "Any chance you could turn the music down a bit?" I said a bit angrily.

"Fuck off, dickhead," he replied and slammed the door shut.

I was fuming. I felt like kicking the door down and giving this arsehole a good thumping, but I couldn't. I would end up getting my license revoked and being put back inside, so I turned and walked back towards my flat door, past the two junkies that were now passed out lying half on and half off the stairs. I just looked at them and was totally disgusted. I closed my door behind me and went and lifted the chair from the living room and jammed it up against the door.

I didn't get much sleep that night and the next day I was knackered but was able to grab a couple of hours' sleep in the evening before I went to work.

9pm and I headed for work. It was a routine that I would get used to and over the next week I just kept my head down and counted the days until payday, which was Friday, and I was never so glad to get my wages as I was totally fleeced and had survived on bread and jam butties for the last two days. So when I went for a grocery shop I treated myself to a sirloin steak and by God, with the pepper sauce and homemade chips it was the nicest dinner I had eaten in a long time.

CHAPTER 3

THE SMELL OF LEATHER

Monday rolled around and at 3pm I had my meeting with Veronica; it only took 15 minutes and as I walked out of that office I wanted to go back and exorcise a few demons so I got a bus to take me to Warrington. On the outskirts of the town there was a house I had recurring nightmares about, and I just wanted them to end.

It took me about an hour on the bus and the closer I got to the town, old memories filled my head, some of which I could never forget and I was angry with myself for not doing something about it a lot earlier in my ruined life.

As I stepped off the bus it was raining so I went into the bus station café and had a bit of dinner and waited for the rain to go off. As I finished of my sandwich I stared into my coffee cup and was just miles away in my own thoughts. I finished the now lukewarm coffee and left to make the 30-minute walk to the house.

It was a good mile or so from anything, up a secluded lane which was now overgrown with just enough room to walk up. As I got to the end of the lane it opened up into a large yard with a couple of old cars that were rotting away over in the corner, and then as I looked at the house it was boarded up, now in a real state of disrepair. As I walked towards it I kicked a vodka bottle out of my way. I went over to the front door and pulled at the wooden board that was nailed to the frame. A couple of good tugs and it broke free. As I stood there looking in to the dark room I was frightened to go in, so I turned and walked back across the yard to find something I could use to pry the boards off the windows to let some light in.

As I looked around I found an old rusty crowbar and then I noticed the burnt ground over by the old shed. I closed my eyes and sighed. I knew what the ash was and as I opened my eyes a tear travelled down my cheek. I wiped it away and went back over to the house.

I wedged the crowbar between the board and frame of the window and pried the board off. The window was broken and the old tattered curtains hung either side of the window. As I looked inside, the place was wrecked; what was left of the furniture was in bits and the smell was overpowering. As I took a breath I coughed at the stench. I decided then that I wasn't going in, there were too many bad memories, so I lifted my lighter out and set fire to the curtains. I stood back and watched as the flames rose up and really took hold. As the room was engulfed in flames I walked backwards and just watched as the house went up. I smiled as the flames rose higher and higher and heat from the flames was now burning my face so I retreated over towards the wreck of a shed. I leaned up against the locked doors and watched as the house slowly collapsed.

I lifted out a cigarette and sparked it up; every draw I took felt good until it was finished but it didn't make me feel any better and the thoughts in my head were as fresh as the day they first happened. I turned and kicked the wooden doors and as one of them came away from its hinges it fell to the ground. I looked inside and just stood there crying. I was overcome with grief and the pain that I felt was just too much. I walked in and into the centre of the room. There, over in the corner was a wooden crate which I turned upright and placed back in the centre of the room so I could stand on it. As I climbed up I could get a better look at the wooden beam that was above me. I reached into my pocket and took out a pen knife. I started carving the names of the kids that had been taken. Angela and Andrew were first, then came Becky and Brian. I carved my own name next and then the last name was Cat.

Cat was my sister who had died when she was only 12. She looked after me and for a good part of my life protected me against the beatings that Joe handed out. I placed my finger on her name, drawing each letter out. The tears were now free flowing down my face. I couldn't take any more of these memories. I just had to end it. I ran my finger over all the names and then as I got to the end of Cat's name there was a large rusty nail half protruding from the beam. I pulled at it but it didn't even budge. I then undid my belt and looped one side through the buckle, creating a noose. I forced one of the holes through the rusty nail and as I placed the noose around my neck I was crying uncontrollably. The years of abuse had taken its toll. I had had enough and just wanted the pain to go away.

I stepped off the box and the noose tightened around my neck. At first I just held my breath but as the pressure built, my eyes started to bulge and I couldn't breathe, but I wanted this to end so I didn't struggle, I just waited to pass out. I closed my eyes and waited. My teeth were clenched together really tightly and my mouth was watering. I was choking out. This was it; the end was close. As I was just about to pass out I heard a voice. It was Cat. I could hear her clearly. She said, "Your name is not Craig and they weren't our mum and dad. We were taken. Go home. Go home to Northern Ireland."

I immediately opened my eyes and pulled at the belt. It broke free and I fell to the ground, hitting my head off the wooden crate and knocking myself out. Everything went dark.

CHAPTER 4

TAKEN

It was 1956. Nigel and Dorothy lived in a town called Newtownards in Northern Ireland. They had two kids – Paula who was 6 years old and Jason who was just 2. They were just a typical wee working-class family trying to do the best for their kids and this is the story of how both their kids were abducted and kept captured for years, never to be found again, and how the kids had to endure abuse from two evil people who brainwashed them into believing that they were their parents.

It was the 4th of July and Dorothy was taking the kids for a week's holiday to her sister's in London. She was going alone as Nigel couldn't get the time off work and she was really nervous about travelling so far with two young kids on her own, but she put a brave face on and as she kissed Nigel on the cheek to say goodbye little did she know what was going to happen.

I sat on my mum's knee on the plane waiting for it to take off and I was so excited as the plane got faster and faster and then it left the ground. I reached across to where Paula was sitting to look out of the window.

"Get away from me," she said and pushed me back.

"Let him see out the window, love," my mum said.

"No, I'm sitting here," Paula said really cheekily.

"Listen here, young madam, you change your attitude or you will not be able to sit down at all."

Paula just put her head down; my mum was usually really quiet but when she told you off you knew not to answer her back. I leaned over and peered out of the small window. I was amazed as the plane got higher and higher and the land got smaller and smaller. Paula just huffed for the rest of the trip, which was around an hour.

When we landed in London city airport it was a bit chaotic. I hadn't seen as many people in one place before and to be honest I was a bit frightened but my mum made Paula hold me tightly as she got our suitcase off the conveyor belt. I wasn't sure who was minding who as I think Paula was a bit scared too.

We left the airport and as we stood at a layby just outside my auntie pulled up in a nice big red car. I think my mum was relieved to see her.

"Hi, love, how was your trip?"

My auntie's name was Gillian. She didn't look anything like my mum; she was a bit younger with long curly hair and glasses but she seemed nice as she stood hugging her.

"Yeah, it was OK, glad it's over to be honest."

"Now who do we have here?" she said as she turned to where Paula and I were.

"I'm Paula and this is Jason," Paula said as she nudged me forward.

"I haven't met you before, son, but I heard all about you and your mum is right, you're a good-looking boy with your nice blond hair and blue eyes, you definitely take your good looks from our side of the family."

She seemed nice as she smiled and kissed me on the head.

"And how are you, Paula, still as cute as ever? You're getting big."

Paula just smiled and put her head down.

We got into my auntie's car and started the drive to her house.

"How's the boys, Gillian?" my mum asked.

"Getting big, our James is in secondary school now and William is in his last year at primary school so hard work with the two of them."

"And what about your Norman, still working away?"

"Yeah, he only gets home one week in five so you won't get to see him as he isn't due home until the end of next week."

"Awk, well sure as long as he is doing well."

The journey to my auntie's house took a good hour and when we arrived it was just like back home, rows of terraced houses with a bit of a front garden; it was a nice area but it wasn't home.

My mum, Paula and I had to share a bedroom as it was a three-bedroom house. My two cousins also had to share a bedroom; they were still at school and didn't get home until after 4.

William came in first as his bus dropped him off right outside the house. He was a big lad and as he came over to where we were sitting watching TV he spoke really funnily.

"I'm William, I'm your big cousin."

I couldn't make him out; he had a funny accent. Paula just smiled at him.

"What is wrong? Has the cat got your tongue?"

"I'm Jason and I am three. Have you got any biscuits?" I loved biscuits, especially the chocolate ones.

"I can do better than that, Jason, come with me."

I followed William to the back hall of the house and as he opened up a large fridge my eyes lit up; there was every bar of chocolate you could think of but my favourite was the Mars bar.

"Take whatever one you want, Jason."

I was straight in there like a shot and grabbed the Mars. William lifted one as well and we snuck out to the back garden and stuffed our faces. I liked William from that moment; he was my key to the fridge and to more Mars bars.

James came home from school just as the dinner was being served. He was a quiet fella, didn't really speak much. He was about the same height as William but not as heavy. He was into his football and played for the local team. Looking at him, I knew he never went into the treasure chest of chocolate that William and I called our secret.

For the next couple of days my auntie took us out to parks and it was OK, but my highlight of the day was when William came home from school and we raided the fridge for chocolate.

Wednesday morning, we had three days left of our holiday. My cousins went to school as usual and my auntie had to go and do some food shopping so my mum told her to go on and she would clean the house for her.

It was a really sunny day. Paula took me out to the front garden and we sat and played with some toys that had belonged to William. My mum nipped in and out to check that we were OK. I think it was that we weren't fighting.

"Are you OK? Do you want some juice?"

"No Mum, we are fine," Paula replied.

"OK love, give me a shout if you need me."

"OK Mum."

She went back into the house and I heard her put the vacuum on; we continued playing in the garden.

As we sat playing a man and woman walked past and then stopped and turned and came back to the garden gate. The man was tall and unshaven, he had a long coat on which I thought was strange as it was really sunny. As for the woman, she was fat and had a flowery dress on. Both her arms had pictures on them. I turned to Paula; she looked frightened. Before I could speak I heard the gate open and I felt two hands around my waist as the woman lifted me. I cried; the look on Paula's face scared me. She started shouting for mum but the man grabbed her and covered her mouth. They walked out of the garden and to a van that was parked down a bit. I struggled to break free but the woman held me so tightly I could barely breathe. I could see Paula being carried; she was kicking and screaming but I couldn't believe what was happening.

As we got to the blue van with windows in the side of it the woman pulled open the side door and got inside with me. It was a strange van. It had flowery seats and a sink and there were curtains across the windows. She sat me at the back of it and told me to be quiet. I just sat there and cried. I wanted my mummy. The man then shoved Paula in and the woman grabbed her and sat her beside me. She cuddled into me, crying. We were so scared.

The man got in and slammed the door. He started the engine and sped off. As we drove past our auntie's house I could see my mum standing in the garden and when I banged the window she saw us. She ran to the gate but the van just kept going. I screamed and so did Paula.

The woman just shouted, "Drive, drive, drive!"

I turned and looked back and I could see my mum running up the street but as the van turned the corner she disappeared and I just banged the windows. The woman smacked me across the legs and told me to sit back down again; I fell to the floor and just curled up in a ball and cried. Again, the woman hit me and told me to be quiet. Paula tried to shield me from the woman but she got hit as well. She fell on top of me and was crying really hard. The woman grabbed her off me by the hair and pushed her back into the seat. As I turned to look at my big sister, the woman had a pair of scissors and started hacking at her hair. Through my tears I could see Paula's hair fall to the floor. I couldn't believe what was happening. I tried to get up but the van was going really fast and I fell against the side of it when it turned a corner.

"Slow down, Joe, you will attract the cops. We have done it, we got them."

Joe turned his head and looked straight at me. "Sit down, boy, before you get hurt."

I stopped crying and just sat beside Paula. She was

still crying. "Don't worry, Mummy will find us," I said.

The woman laughed. "I'm your mummy now."

Joe turned around. "And I'm your daddy." He laughed when he said that. I was so scared and by the look on Paula's face so was she.

When the woman stopped cutting Paula's hair it was so short; she was still crying and put her arms around me but the woman prised her from me, hitting her a couple of times, and then cut my hair. I'd never liked getting my hair cut but this time I didn't flinch, I just focused on Paula and could see her mouthing the words, "Don't move. Don't move." So I didn't.

Snip, snip, snip. I could hear the sound of the scissors and could see my blond hair falling around me. She didn't stop until all of my hair was cut off; she then pushed me towards Paula and said, "Now you two wee pets be quiet. It won't be long until we are home."

I cuddled into Paula.

It was a long time. I had fallen asleep and so had Paula. We were woken up when the woman shook us. "Right, you two, wake up, we are home." At first I thought I had had a bad dream but it became real when I realised where we were and who we were with. I held Paula's hand as the woman opened the door of the van.

I could see a house and a big shed and lots of trees. There were two other cars there parked side by side, and then the man came to the door. I took a deep breath. Paula pulled me back into the van. "Take us home, please take us home!" she cried.

"Now, now, you are home. GET OUT OF THE VAN!" he shouted.

His voice was frightening. We both got out. "Now get into the house." He pushed us forward. We stumbled.

The woman came and held my hand. She bent down. "It will be OK. I'm sure you are hungry, my wee pet?"

I looked at her hard. She scared me. She had long greasy hair and bad teeth; her breath was stinking. I coughed. She had hairs on her chin and as she kissed me on the forehead I could feel them scratching my face. Paula pushed her away. "Don't you dare kiss him."

She slapped Paula hard across the face and she fell to the mucky ground. "You will learn your place here, madam." She grabbed my arm and marched me into the house. As we went through the front door she brought me into a room at the back of the house and pushed me in and closed the door behind me. I stood there crying. I wanted Paula, I wanted my mummy. A few minutes passed and then the door opened and Paula was pushed in. Her nose was bleeding and she was crying. I ran over and just hugged her. She held me really tightly.

"I will bring you some dinner, now just be quiet or Joe will use his belt on you both." The door was closed again.

We stood there holding each other in a dimly lit room. There were two beds over on one side of it but the window that separated them was boarded up so we couldn't see outside. "Jason, you have to be quiet," Paula said to me, holding my face. "You have to be a good boy or that man will hurt you, do you understand me?"

I nodded and wiped my tears away. From that moment I knew I would never see my mummy or daddy again.

The door opened again and the women came in with two bowls. "Right, you two, here is your dinner. Eat it all up or Joe will be angry."

It was like a stew, I think, and it was revolting but Paula made me eat it as she knew what would happen if I didn't.

After a while the woman came back in again. "Right, you two, did you eat it all up?"

"Yes, we did," Paula replied.

"Bath time." She turned and we followed her out into the living room where in the centre of the room was a big bath filled with water and bubbles. We both just stood and looked at it.

"Get undressed," the man said as he sat in a chair in the corner of the room rocking back and forth.

Paula held my hand really tightly.

"Are you two deaf? Get your clothes off and get into the bath." He was getting really aggressive when he said that.

We both started crying and Paula said, "Please take us home, please, please take us home."

He came walking towards us. Paula held me. He hit us with his belt and it hurt, really hurt. The woman grabbed him and told him to stop. She then undressed us both and as we stood there naked I could see welt marks on Paula. She was still crying and so was I. The woman lifted Paula first and put her in the bath, then she lifted me an set me in beside her. I winced in pain. The water wasn't that warm but she washed both of us with a face cloth and then lifted Paula out first and wrapped her in a towel. The man lifted me out and wrapped me in a towel. He dried me and then handed me a pair of jammies. The woman dried Paula and handed her jammies as well. "Put these on you and it's off to bed for the two of you." Paula took me by the hand and we went into the bedroom. She closed the door behind us and put me into one of the beds. She got in beside me and we cried ourselves to sleep.

We weren't allowed to leave the house for days. It was the same routine – brought out from our room for food and then put back in again. At night time I could hear the man and woman argue and at times I think he hit her as I could hear her crying.

CHAPTER 5

RUN FOR YOUR LIFE

A few months had passed and the only time we got outside was when the man went into town to get groceries so the woman let us go outside and play. She came outside with us and just watched as we took turns on an old tyre that was suspended from a tree by a tattered rope. It was really good fun and I laughed really hard when Paula had her turn and when she got off she was really dizzy and kept falling over. It was one of the times that we forgot where we were, and were just kids having fun.

It never lasted long. We were taken back into the house and put back in the bedroom before Joe got back. We were told to call them by their names – the woman was called Mary and we were also renamed. I was now called Craig and Paula was called Catherine but it was shortened to Cat. We grew to accept it as if we didn't we both knew it was a few hits with a belt, or whatever Joe had close to hand.

After months of living here our previous life was just a distant memory and I think even Cat had now accepted this life. We still sometimes cried ourselves to sleep but less and less, unlike the constant beatings we took from Joe when he was drunk, and then it began.

It was a Saturday afternoon. It was a really lovely warm day and Joe was away to get drunk. Mary let us play outside, a game of hide and seek, but it was cut short when Cat went a little bit too far down the laneway and Mary shouted at her to get back into the house. She was quite angry at her and give her a slap. I just stood there and watched as Mary pulled Cat by the hair, swearing at her and trailing her into the house but Cat didn't even shed a tear and neither did I, I think we were used to the beatings or just didn't have any more tears to cry.

We were kept in the room for the next few hours and that's where we were given our dinner.

Later on that evening we heard Joe come in. He was really drunk as he was shouting at Mary, wanting his dinner. "Where is my dinner?"

Mary always gave him as good as she took. "Where have you been all this time?"

"Just shut your mouth and get me my dinner, woman."

"Who do you think you're talking to?"

It then kicked off. We heard furniture being knocked over and Mary screaming as Joe laid into her and it went on for a few minutes and then it went silent.

Cat and I hid under the bed; we had pulled the blankets down a bit to cover where we were. We peered out, watching and listening. We could hear Mary sobbing and then we looked as we saw the old rusted round handle turn and the door being opened. We slid back under the bed right up against the wall. Cat put her finger up to her mouth. "Shhh!"

She then put her arm around me and pulled me in

close. We waited and watched.

We could see Joe's dirty old boots as he paced up and down the room. "Where are you, you wee bitch?" he said as he pulled the blankets off the beds. I was scared. Was he going to beat us again? I closed my eyes and held my breath, hoping he would go away. Cat held me really tightly. I could hear the wardrobe being pulled open and Joe pulling clothes off the wire hangers looking for us. I exhaled and opened my eyes; I saw Joe's boots turn and could now see him standing facing where we were hiding. He walked forwards. His boots were now partially under the bed. We waited and watched.

He started walking backwards. We both exhaled at the same time. I don't know about Cat but my heart was thumping. I closed my eyes slowly and just breathed; when I opened my eyes I screamed. Joe grabbed me and pulled me out.

"There you are, you wee fucker." He threw me across the room and then grabbed Cat.

"Come here, you wee bitch." Cat was screaming and tried to fight him off but he was far too strong and he trailed her out from beneath the bed. Her screams were deafening as she tried in vain to avoid his grip. I got up and ran over to help her but by now she was in his grasp and he was back on his feet again. He lifted his leg and just shoved me away with his boot. He kicked me so hard I fell against the wardrobe and was knocked unconscious.

The next thing I knew I was back in bed. I opened my eyes and looked across to where Cat's bed was. She was lying crying. I got out of bed and went over.

"Cat, are you OK?"

She turned and looked at me; her face was marked but as she wiped her tears away she said, "We have to run away, Craig, we have to run away."

"No, Cat, we can't. What happened?"

"I don't want to talk about it." Tears travelled down her cheeks.

I put my arm around her. "Did he hurt you, Cat?"

The door starting creaking as it was being opened. I scurried back into bed and pulled the covers over my head.

I heard someone walk across the floor and then my blankets were pulled back.

"Are you OK, son?"

I opened my eyes. Mary was standing over me; she was crying.

"Yes I am but Cat isn't."

She turned and walked over to Cat. I watched as she pulled the blankets off her and was really terrified when I saw Cat's nightdress covered in blood.

"Oh my god, are you OK?"

Cat just lay there crying.

"I will be back in a minute," Mary said as she turned and walked out of the room.

I got out of bed and went over to Cat.

"What did he do to you, Cat?"

Cat wiped her tears away.

"He is an evil man, Craig. He hurt me. We have to get out of here, we have to run away." Just as Cat said that Mary returned and she had heard everything. She stomped across the room and threw a clean nightdress at Cat.

"Any more of that talk and I will get the belt for

both of you, now get yourself changed and get to bed." She turned and slammed the door behind her. I heard the key turn in the lock and again we were prisoners.

I hugged Cat.

"What are we going to do, Cat?"

"Nothing, Craig, we are stuck here." Cat got changed and got back into bed. I got back into my bed and I just lay there listening to Cat cry herself to sleep.

I knew then, that night, we had to plan to get away. If we stayed he would end up killing us so I lay and plotted a way out.

We didn't see Joe for over a week. We really hoped he would never come back but come back he did, stinking of drink and as abusive as ever, especially to Mary who took the brunt of it, but he took himself off to bed and just stayed there for a couple of days, only coming out to grunt for food and hurl abuse at us.

Cat and I had made plans that the next time we were out in the yard and Joe was away getting shopping, that we would make a run for it, but we had to wait for the right moment.

It was a Saturday afternoon. We heard Joe tell Mary that he was going into town for messages and he would be away for a couple of hours. We knew that was his excuse to go and get drunk and that he would come home and start on either Mary or us so we decided today was the day to escape. Cat was really scared he would take her into the room again so she kept whispering to me, "We have to go. We have to go today."

Joe left and Mary made us lunch. I swear I couldn't

eat a bite, I was so scared, but knew we had to go.

"Can we go out and play, Mary?" Cat asked.

"Not today, I'm too tired, you both can go for a sleep as well."

"But I want to go out and play!" Cat said quite loudly.

Mary took a step towards her and slapped her across the face. Cat fell to the ground but got up as quick as she fell and ran towards me and grabbed my hand.

"Run, Craig. Run!"

I didn't even have time to think; she pulled me towards the front door and just as she got the door open for us to get out Mary grabbed my other arm.

"Where are you going?" she screamed.

"Let him go!" Cat shouted. "Let him go!"

One good tug and Mary had me in her grasp. Cat just kept running. I screamed, "Cat!"

She turned and looked but she just kept running. Mary threw me into the room and locked the door. I screamed again. "Cat!" I heard the front door being slammed shut.

As Cat ran down the lane Mary followed.

*

My heart was thumping. I just kept saying. "Craig, I will get help." I kept running.

I could hear Mary behind me. "Get back here, you wee bitch."

I could see the end of the lane. I was nearly there. "Stop now!" she shouted at me.

My heart was racing. I could hardly breathe. I was free.

I ran out onto the road. I stopped to look to see which way to run. I turned to see where Mary was and then I heard screeching of tyres. I turned again only to be hit by Joe's van. The last thing I heard was a big bang and a flash of white light and then it went black.

As I slowly opened my eyes, I was in the arms of Joe. I could see his mouth moving but couldn't hear a thing. I floated in and out of consciousness. My eyes closed then when they opened again I was lying on the sofa in the house. I could barely see; everything was blurry. I struggled to breathe. I could feel what I thought was water running out of my mouth. I coughed slightly but didn't have the strength to spit the fluid from my mouth. I closed my eyes again. I could see a blurred figure standing in the distance; it was a woman. She held her hand out and I could hear her saying, "It's OK, pet, come with me, you're safe now." I smiled and took her hand and walked with her.

"What have you done, Joe? You have killed her!"

"How was this my fault? It was your stupid fault, you let her out." Joe punched Mary in the face, knocking her to the ground. "You're lucky I did hit her or the police would be here, you stupid bitch." He laid into Mary, kicking her repeatedly.

*

I hid under my bed, crying. "Cat, where are you?" I said through my tears.

I could hear the screams and yells of Mary as Joe give her a bad beating and then it went all silent.

I waited a while and then came out from under my bed. I slowly tried the door but it was locked tight so

I went over to the small hole in the wall and peered through to see if I could see anything outside.

I saw Joe go into the big shed and he carried out some wood. He piled it up in the middle of the yard and then went back into the shed where he came out with a large container. He emptied some of the contents onto the wood, set it down and then went back into the shed. A couple of minutes passed but when he came out he was carrying an old rolled up rug. He walked over to the pile of wood and set it on top and poured the rest of the contents of the container onto it. I watched on as he went into the pocket of his old ripped jeans and took out his lighter. He bent down and set light to a corner of the rug. I watched on as the flames engulfed the rug and wood, but then I heard Mary scream and watched as she ran over to the fire, but Joe held her back. She was hitting him but Joe just kept pushing her back and I could hear him saying, "It's the only way, I will get you another one."

Mary fell to the ground with her head in her hands. I watched on and then I could see what Joe's fire was burning. I turned away and screamed, "Cat!" I watched as the rug burned away, revealing Cat's body. I turned away and held my head in my hands. I screamed at the realisation that my sister was dead and that he was burning her. I crawled under my bed and curled up in a wee ball. I couldn't breathe. I cried and cried and cried. I didn't want to come out from beneath that bed. I was so scared that Joe would kill me too.

They left me in that room for a long time, maybe two days, I think, and when Mary came in she struggled to walk. I could see that she was covered in bruises and her clothes were stained with blood. Joe had given her a really bad beating. She was carrying a bowl and a glass of water. She set it down on the small bedside table and just turned and walked out. I didn't say a thing, I just watched as she closed and locked the door behind her.

I was starving. I lifted the bowl and ate the contents in a flash. It wasn't great but it filled my empty belly. I sat on my bed and drank the water. I was still struggling to come to terms with the fact that Joe had killed Cat. I was alone and frightened and trapped.

After a while I felt so tired and dizzy that I went to stand up but couldn't; I fell back onto the bed and it went dark.

I didn't get to leave that room for days and the only time the door was opened was when Mary brought me something to eat. I even had to piss through the hole in the wall but had no other option but to crap in the corner when I needed to go. I got used to the smell and to be honest I really didn't care anymore, I just wanted to die.

After a couple of weeks I was really weak and sleeping most of the time. It got to the stage that I didn't know what day it was. I had just given up. I went to sleep again.

I don't know how long I lay there but when I came round I was in the back of Joe's van and Mary was brushing my hair. I could see trees and hedges through the windows and was really confused. I tried to sit up but Mary held me down. "It's OK, love, we are just going a drive. Everything is OK."

Was this real or a dream? I closed my eyes tightly

and then opened them again. It was real. I could see the back of Joe's head as he drove the van. He looked around at me. "Back with the living then." He laughed and turned back again.

"That's enough, Joe, he has been through enough."

"Don't you start, woman, or I won't get you another one."

"Sorry Joe," Mary said as she kept brushing my hair.

Another one, I thought. *What is he talking about?*

We must have driven for a good hour but then we stopped and Joe got out. Again, I tried to sit up but Mary pinned me down. "Just lie down, my wee pet. Joe is getting you a wee sister." My eyes widened; my heart was racing.

The side door of the van was flung open and Mary's grip on me loosened. I sat up. Joe got in carrying this wee girl. She was no more than about two and she was screaming. He gave her to Mary and slammed the door shut. I saw him run round to the front of the van and get in. Mary pushed me back into a seat and held the wee girl down as Joe sped off.

"What have you done? Let her go. She is only a baby!" I screamed.

Mary turned and hit me. "Sit down and shut up."

I knew what was coming so I cowered away in to the corner and just watched each street as we passed, and then it was countryside and then it was the lane way and back to the house. I knew then what had happened. I knew in that instant I should have tried to escape, but there was this little girl now and she would need someone to try and keep her safe and away from Joe.

CHAPTER 6

DOROTHY

I dragged my feet as I walked behind Mary who was carrying the wee girl who was still crying. I could hear Joe walking behind me, or should I say I could smell him; his odour was overpowering at times and this was one of those times. He stank.

"Hurry up, Craig, get into the house," he growled at me as he hit me with a boot on the backside. I ran on into the house and out of his grasp and straight into my room and I closed the door behind me. I lay on my bed listening to Joe and Mary make a fuss over this child.

"Come on now, wee pet, stop crying," Mary said in a calming voice.

"She is quiet pretty, isn't she Mary?" Joe said.

"You leave her alone, Joe, she is only a baby."

"You would say that. I'm away for a drink."

I could hear it all and was glad when I heard the front door being slammed shut. I went to my piss hole and peered out.

I saw Joe turn the van in the yard and then drive off. I went out to the living room where Mary was trying to console the wee girl. I walked over and stood beside her.

"This is Dorothy, your wee sister, Craig." The name struck a chord with me. I had heard that name before but didn't know where.

I looked at her; she was still crying. I wiped her tears away. She looked up at me and put her arms out. I didn't know what to do I took a step back.

"Don't be like that, Craig, she just wants you to hold her."

I stepped forward and lifted her. She put her arms round my neck and held on really tightly. She cuddled into me.

"She likes you, Craig."

I had to protect her. "Bo Bo," she said. I didn't know what she wanted. I looked at Mary. "What does she want?"

"She wants her bottle. Hold on, I will make her one up." Mary got up and went over to the fridge.

"Bo Bo," she repeated.

"It's coming now," I replied as I cuddled her back.

I looked over at Mary where she was heating a saucepan of water and set a bottle of milk into the now bubbling water.

"It's OK, wee Dot, your Bo Bo is coming now," I said as I cuddled this little girl.

She put her hand on my cheek and said, "Bo Bo."

"Yes, it's coming now."

God love her, she smiled at me, her wee eyes all red with crying.

Mary came over and sat down. "Give her to me, son."

I set her on Mary's knee, who then began to give Dot her Bo Bo.

She drank it in a flash and by the end of the bottle she was sleeping. Mary got up with Dot in her arms and walked into my bedroom and put her in Cat's bed. I gave a big sigh and dropped my head. I was in such pain from losing my sister. If I was going to escape this was the perfect opportunity. I turned and walked towards the front door and as I put my hand on the rusty handle I took a deep breath. I couldn't go. I had to look after this wee child and try and keep Joe away from her.

I turned and walked into my bedroom. Mary was just getting up from putting Dot to bed. "Why don't you get your head down for an hour, son? It's been a long day."

"I think I will," I replied.

As Mary closed the door behind me I could hear the key turn and I was a prisoner again. I lay on my bed just looking over at Dot. She was sound asleep. God love her, she was so innocent and I began to think about her real mum and dad and how they would be feeling at losing their wee daughter. I feared what the future would bring.

I must have fallen asleep as I was woken with the door being flung open and there stood a drunken Joe. "Come here, you," he said to me in an aggressive manner. I got out of bed and walked towards him.

"What is it Joe?" I asked worriedly.

He grabbed me by the back of my jumper and pulled me out into the living room.

"Make me a cup of tea and something to eat."

"OK, Joe. OK."

His grasp loosened and I went over to the kettle and filled it with water. I lit the gas ring and set the kettle on to boil. I then lifted a couple of rounds of bread out of the bread basket and buttered them. I went into the fridge to see what I could get to make a sandwich. There wasn't much there. I lifted a block of cheese which by the looks of it must have been there for a while as there were blue spots on it. I lifted a knife and cut a couple of slices of it and set them on one of the bits of bread and then put the other slice on top and cut it in half. The whistle of the kettle started so I turned the gas ring off and made him a cup of tea. "I will take a mug of tea as well, Craig," Mary said.

I lifted another cup from the shelf and made her tea. I gave Joe his nice blue mould cheese sandwich and his tea and then gave Mary hers.

"That's not a bad sandwich, Craig, we will make a cook out of you yet," Joe said, slurring his words.

I just thought, *I hope it poisons you,* and then replied, "Thanks."

I could hear Dot crying. "I will get her," I said to Mary.

"I hope this one isn't a crier, Mary, like them other two we had."

"Joe, shut up," Mary said quite quickly.

As I walked into the bedroom my mind was racing. *Other two?* I thought. *Holy shit, there have been kids before me and Cat.* I walked slowly to Dot's bed. She was sitting up and had her arms outstretched, and then I realised that all the clothes I had been given must have belonged to another boy. I lifted Dot and went over to the wardrobe and opened it up. I looked hard at the piles of clothes. Some were for boys, some were for girls and they all had one thing in common –

they were all threadbare. These clothes were years old. *Oh my god, how many kids have they taken?* I thought. *And worst of all, MURDERED.* I took a deep breath and held Dot tightly. "I won't let them hurt you, wee pet," I said softly into her ear.

"Bring Dorothy out here, Craig," Mary said.

I walked out with her in my arms.

"Give her to me," Joe said.

My eyes widened. I walked straight over to Mary and set her on her knee.

"I said give her to me," Joe repeated really angrily.

"It's OK, Joe, she is fine here, aren't you my wee Dorothy?" Mary said.

"You have named her already," Joe said as he stood up. "Do I not even get a say? You named the other ones as well."

"Other ones," I said out loud (that was a big mistake). The next thing I knew Joe had punched me and I fell to the ground. He laid into me with his boot. I tried to protect myself by crawling under the table but he grabbed me by the ankles and trailed me out and kicked me again. I just curled up in a ball and took it. I could hear Mary squealing at him to get him to stop and he only did 'cause he was out of breath. I staggered to my feet and went into my room and closed the door behind me. I didn't cry; I was used to his beatings. I sat with my back to the door and I could hear him arguing with Mary. He wanted to take Dot to his room but Mary wouldn't let him. I heard her say she would rather die first than hand this one over.

"Fuck you, Mary," he said and he slammed the front door on the way out. I crawled over on my hands and knees to the piss hole and looked out. He got into his van and started it up. I watched as he turned it in the yard and pointed it at the house. He revved and revved the engine and then took off. I fell backwards as I thought he was going to drive the van right into the house but he must have swerved at the last minute 'cause I could hear him driving away.

I went back into the living room where Mary was nursing Dot with another bottle. She looked at me. "You should know better than to talk back to Joe, you know he has a temper."

"I know but tell me, how many kids have you had?"

She looked at me. "A few."

"A few! How many is a few?"

"Dot is number seven," she replied.

I was shocked. "Seven? Where did they go?"

"As I said, Joe has a temper, now forget about it."

"What were their names?"

"Promise me you won't tell Joe when he comes back?"

"I won't." My heart was racing. I couldn't even feel the pain anymore, I just wanted to know their names.

"The first two were called Angela and Andrew but they didn't last long, six months or so, then you had Becky and Brian, they were good kids, they didn't give us any trouble. We had them for over a year, and then we got you and your sister. I told Joe just to take you but he wanted her and look where that has brought us, to this wee pet, Dorothy."

I stood with my mouth open. "Seven kids, seven,"

I repeated.

"I won't let Joe hurt this wee one," she said as she talked into Dot's face.

Yeah right, I thought. *When you get bored with her Joe will take her.*

I don't know why but I walked over to the cooker, lifted the rusty old frying pan, turned and walked over to behind Mary and hit her such a crack on the head with it, she fell to the floor still holding Dot, who was now squealing. I quickly lifted her and as I lifted her bottle off the floor I could see blood start to run from Mary's head. There was a lot of it. "Come on, Dot, we are getting out of here." We left that house under the cover of darkness. I had never been so frightened but knew I couldn't let Mary and Joe hurt this wee child.

CHAPTER 7

LIVING ROUGH

I was twelve when I escaped with Dot. That night, I would keep with me forever. We hid about half a mile away in an old deserted factory waiting for the sun to come up. It was a long night. It felt like an eternity but when it did rise I just kept off the main road and stuck to the fields. I walked for a couple of hours and came across a church. I checked the doors but it was locked. We stayed for a while there but Dot was hungry and began to cry. She had already drunk what was left of her bottle but was starving. I was hungry too but just had to keep going. As I walked across another field I didn't know what time it was, I just knew we were both cold and hungry. I could see what I thought was a small school. As I got closer there was a car parked and one of the rooms had a light on so I knew someone was there. I walked over to the door and tried it; it was open as I walked into the hallway. I could feel that it was nice and warm. I heard a voice. "Is that you, Jane?"

I panicked. Dot started crying. I hugged her and said, "It's for the best." I kissed her on the head and sat her down in the hallway.

"Hey, you, what are you doing?" the voice said.

I looked up and there was this woman standing not too far from me. I looked at her as she looked at me then I just turned and ran away. "Stop! Stop! Come back here."

I just kept running; I ran until I could run no more and just sat with my back against a tree. "What now?" I said. "What are you going to do now? You can't go back."

I got up and started walking; I hadn't a clue where I was going or what I was going to do but anything would be better than going back and any way, if she was dead then I would go to jail and then there was Joe. If he found me I'd be dead anyway.

I walked for hours and I was absolutely starving. I eventually came into a built up area. I walked through the streets; there were houses and some shops and as I walked past a shop that had some fruit and vegetables outside it I stole a bunch of bananas and took to my heels and ran. I heard someone shout at me but I ran on and hid around the back of a couple of houses. I sat quietly and ate the bananas and just listened for anyone coming, which they didn't. I was relieved not only for not getting caught but to get something to eat. I sat for a while and then walked through the back alleyways of the streets to stay out of sight.

Walking through what I now knew was Liverpool City Centre, I looked into each shop window. I was frightened and hungry again and tired. I sat down in an entrance of a shop that had closed down. I could feel the cold through my threadbare jeans; I was shivering. I just sat with my knees up to my chest and my arms wrapped around my legs. I had my hoody pulled up over my head to try and keep warm but it was no use, I was freezing and now shaking uncontrollably.

As I sat there feeling sorry for myself a passer-by stopped. "Are you OK?" the voice said.

I looked up and through my tears I saw a man standing in front of me. I didn't answer, I just shook my head.

"Are you lost?" he said.

Again, I just shook my head.

"Have you had anything to eat?"

"No," I replied, wiping my tears away.

He reached into his pocket and handed me two pounds. "Here, get yourself something to eat, son."

I took the money from him. "Thank you," I replied and quickly put the money in my pocket. The man then walked away.

I got up from that doorway and walked back down the road where I had passed a McDonald's and got myself a breakfast meal. Well, it wasn't a meal, I could only get the burger but got 45p change. I sat there for a good hour or so just to keep warm and then went to the bathroom where I was able to get a drink of water and go to the toilet which took me another 30 minutes or so as I was able to lock the door and just stay warm. After the 3rd person had rapped the door I left.

Walking about Liverpool, I felt so alone. This was a big place and I was only a boy.

I found another abandoned shop front so I hunkered down in one of the corners to get out of the now pouring rain. As I sat watching the water run by my thoughts were now on where I was going to sleep tonight and how I was going to keep warm.

I don't know how long I sat there but it was starting to get dark. My stomach was rumbling. I needed to get going again; this doorway was too exposed, I needed somewhere more secluded and away from the main road.

The rain was easing but without a coat it didn't take long for my clothes to be soaked through. I was so cold and my whole body was shaking uncontrollably.

As I walked up one of the back alleys a door opened not far in front of me. I stood my ground and just watched as a man came out carrying a black bin. He walked over to a larger green skip-type bin and emptied the contents of his black bin into it, and then went back in through the door he came from. I walked up to the green bin and lifted the lid. To my amazement it was nearly full of discarded food. I plundered through some of it and found a bit of chicken and some chips – *Beggars can't be choosers,* I thought – and just starting eating. It wasn't warm but it wasn't freezing either so it did the job and I was full. I also found a half bottle of water so I took my fill and washed the not-too-bad chicken and chips down.

I walked up the next alleyway and at the end of it there was a wooden fence that had partially rotted away. As I pulled at one of the boards it came free so I squeezed through and was now in a bit of a yard. There were some pallets in one corner and over by a loading bay there were some cardboard boxes and some old covers. I had an idea.

I pulled pallet after pallet over to the corner of the

yard and around a corner away from prying eyes. I wedged two of them against a wall and another two side by side leaning against the two I had just placed. I then went and got the covers and placed them over the pallets to make a shelter. I finished it off with nearly all the cardboard boxes by breaking them down and placing them in the inside to make a bit of a mattress. As I crawled through the gap I had left I used one of the covers as a pillow and another couple as blankets. It wasn't too bad; at least it was dry and was warmer than sleeping in a doorway.

I dozed in and out of consciousness but to be honest it was the best night's sleep I'd had in a very long time and during my time here this was to be my home for a few months.

I got into a routine of walking the streets during the day figuring out where to get free food and the best spots to beg for spare cash, which enabled me to buy a coat and some other bits and pieces out of a charity shop. I also got into the habit of lifting the stuff people donated to the shops before they opened. A good time to do this was around 8.15am, especially the one up at the shopping centre as people dropped bags off before going to work.

Mondays were the best. You always got good stuff then. Anything I couldn't use myself I tried to pawn at the local pawn shop which was always good for electrical equipment – you would sometimes get 2 or 3 quid for a half decent toaster or kettle, so when I was able to get these items my eyes would light up because I knew I would eat well that day.

One night I came back after a good day's begging to my home gone. I stood there looking at the place where my bed had been and there was just nothing. My heart sank and to make matters worse the rain came on.

I looked around the yard to see where my stuff I had gathered over the last couple of months had gone, but it was useless. I had nothing again except the wet clothes I now stood in.

I walked over to the loading bay just to get out of the rain and as I sat against the old rusty shutter I tried to figure out where I was going to get my head down for the night. I went through my pockets to count what money I had and six pounds, fifty-six pence was all that I had in the world.

As I stood up I fell against the shutter door which made a loud noise and that's when I noticed a large black dog staring straight at me.

I put my hand out to greet it and said, "Hello there. Aren't you a big boy?"

The dog just stood there and growled. "Come on now, I won't hurt you." Again I held my hand out.

The dog took a few steps forward and this time it barked at me which made me jump. It growled again; I knew then that I was in trouble.

I looked over to the part of the fence that I used to get in and out and then looked back at the dog which was now growling very loudly. I was petrified of this thing; it was bloody huge and I could see it baring its teeth. I started walking sideways towards my escape route but the dog then took a charge at me. I took to my heels but as I got to the fence the dog grabbed me by the leg and by God did it hurt. I fell to the ground with the dog now shaking me very violently. I was on my back trying to kick the thing off but the more I kicked at it the more it shook me.

One good kick connected to the dog's head and it released its grip. I shuffled backwards on my backside towards the fence; the dog came at me again. As I got to the fence I slid the board over a bit and tried to shuffle through but the dog had me in its grasp again. I could feel it bite hard on my foot and it tried to drag me back into the yard. This thing was going to kill me. I tried in vain to break free but it was no use, it pulled and pulled until it was dragging me back in through the fence. I was scraping at the ground but still I was being dragged by the dog.

As I was now screaming for help, the dog was going to town on me, biting through my trainers and piercing my skin. The pain was horrific. I squealed.

As I turned to face the dog, kicking it again in the head, I was in a fight for my life as it had the taste of blood and was going to finish me off.

Just as I thought I was done for I lifted a piece of wood that was lying beside me and hit the dog with an almighty crack across the head. The dog yelped and let go of my foot and staggered back a bit. The piece of wood was stuck to the side of its head and I watched as the dog fell to the ground.

I sat and watched as the dog was shaking and then it lay still; everything was silent, only the sound of the rain as it hit the puddles that had formed around me and the now dead dog. I got to my feet and limped over to where the dog was and as I stared at it I could feel the pain in my foot and leg take hold and I was in agony. I limped over to the fence and climbed through, pulling the board back to hide my escape.

I staggered down the alleyway and out on to the

main road and got in to the nearest shop front that was vacant to assess my injuries.

I slumped down against one of the walls and lifted the leg of my now ripped jeans to see what damage the dog had done. I wiped what blood there was away using some rain water from a busted pipe and could see a couple of puncture marks where the dog had bitten me. My trainer was missing and when I removed my blood-filled sock my foot had two gashes down the side of it and the blood was oozing from it. I held it really tightly and the pain was unbearable. I was in a mess and didn't know how to fix it. I sat there crying not only in pain but I was as low as I had ever been and felt like giving up.

"Are you OK, son?" a voice said in front of me.

I looked up to see two people standing in high-vis jackets; it was the police.

I let go of my foot to wipe the tears from my eyes. "No, I'm hurt," I replied.

"Oh my goodness, you're in a bit of a mess, son," one of the men said as he bent down to see me.

The other policeman lifted his radio from his lapel. "I need an ambulance dispatched immediately to Lime Street. I have a young male with multiple lacerations."

The operator replied, "I will get that dispatched straight away. Any other assistance needed?"

"No, it's a single male, just get the response here as quick as you can, he is losing a lot of blood, possible artery ruptured."

"It's on its way."

The officer that was now crouched down beside me said, "What happened to you, son?"

"I was attacked by a dog," I replied through my tears.

He stood up and took his belt off.

I raised my hands to protect my head. "Don't, don't hit me," I pleaded.

"Wow, you are OK, son. I'm not going to hit you, I need to stop the blood," the officer said in a calming voice.

I lowered my hands, he then crouched down beside me again and put the belt round just below my knee and fastened it really tightly.

"I'm sorry, son, if it hurts, but I have to stop the bleeding until the ambulance arrives."

I just looked at him and then felt really dizzy and everything went dark.

I had lived on the streets of Liverpool for just over two years. The summer months were enjoyable and begging was easy – they were when I was mostly at ease, but the winter months were the hardest with the sleet and snow. I felt at times I just wanted the cold to take me so it maybe was a godsend when that dog attacked me.

CHAPTER 8

MEALS ON WHEELS

I woke up feeling nice and warm. I was in a bed with proper blankets. As I looked around I realised I was in a hospital ward. There were three other people in beds, all old people, but this was a huge improvement to living on the streets.

I lifted the covers off to look at my leg and foot but they were bandaged up so I couldn't see what damage had been done, so I just pulled the nice warm blankets back over me and up under my chin. This was heaven. I didn't even mind the dull pain in my leg, I just lay there in pure comfort.

I must have dozed off again because I was woken up with the sound of a girl's voice.

"Hello, would you like some tea and toast?"

I sat up. *Jesus,* I thought. *I am in heaven.* "Yes please," I replied.

She pulled over a table on wheels which was now in front of me; she then set down two rounds of toast and a wee tub of butter and jam and a cup of tea. I was in awe at this.

She set down a piece of paper with a pen. "Can you fill this in for me? It's what you would like for your lunch and dinner. I will get it off you when you finish your breakfast."

My eyes widened. "Yes, I definitely will," I said. Eager to see what my choices were, I lifted the paper. It read: tomato or chicken soup, ham and cheese sandwich or tuna and onion and then rice pudding.

I lifted the pen and just ticked it all. I really didn't care what I got but secretly hoped to get it all.

For dinner it was potatoes and chicken with vegetables and gravy with cake and custard to follow. I licked my lips at the thought of it.

I set it back down again and buttered my toast, putting all the jam on it. As I bit into it, I couldn't remember the last time that I had tasted anything so nice. The tea was lovely and warm and the combination of both was just perfect.

Half an hour or so passed and the girl returned. "Did you enjoy that?" she asked.

"Indeed I did. That was the nicest tea and toast I have ever tasted."

As she lifted my lunch and dinner order she looked at me and smiled. "Think you're a bit of a chancer," she said as she laughed.

"God loves a tryer," I replied, smiling back at her.

"I will see what I can do," she said as she lifted my plate and cup and set them on her trolley.

"Thanks," I said as she walked away.

I had another wee sleep and thought to myself that I wanted to stay here forever. It was the first time I had felt safe and most of all, warm.

After I had my lunch the doctor came and saw me to explain what they had done and how long I was expected to stay in. Two days was all I was going to get and after that I wasn't sure where I was going to go or sleep.

The next day I was visited by a policeman.

"Hello, I am Constable John Patterson. Can you tell me your name and address please?"

"Hello, my name is Craig. I don't have an address, I live on the streets."

"I'm sorry to hear that, Craig, I never caught your surname."

"I don't have one," I replied.

"You don't have one? Everyone has a surname"

"I just don't have one. I'm just called Craig."

The policeman took out a note book and pen and wrote something down.

"OK, son, and how old are you?"

"I'm fifteen, sir."

Again he wrote that down.

"And where have you been living?"

"I have been staying here and there. Wherever I can, to be honest."

"And for how long have you been living rough, then?"

"I think it's a couple of years now," I said, a bit concerned, wondering where he was going with this.

"Where did you live before?"

I panicked and started stuttering. "I had to leave, I had to leave, he was hitting me."

"Calm down, Craig, you're safe now," he said. "Look, you're obviously upset. I will come back later and speak a bit more."

"OK," I replied and gave a sigh of relief.

After the policeman left I was really worried he would find out that I had killed Mary and I would go to jail, so I decided I would have to leave but not until after I got my dinner.

As I sat up in bed eating my potatoes and chicken the old fella opposite me spoke.

"Slow down there, young fella, you will get indigestion."

I looked up and smiled as I shovelled the rest of the chicken into my mouth.

"There is no shortage of food in here, son. Take your time. For goodness' sake if you're that hungry you can have mine as well."

"I have to go, I can't stay here," I replied.

"Are you in trouble, son?"

"You could say that."

"I am saying that. Why do you have to leave?" The old man was worse than the policeman.

"I just have to go before he comes back,"

"Oh, right, the less said the better then." The old man seemed nice.

I finished off my dinner and after the girl took the empty plates away I was to make my escape.

I got out of bed and pulled the curtain round. I then looked for my clothes but they were gone. I searched and searched but I had nothing to wear, only the blue pyjamas that they had put me in. I pulled the curtain back and there stood the policeman with a nurse and another woman who was dressed in a suit and had glasses on.

"Going somewhere, Craig?" the policeman asked.

"No, no, just wanted a bit of privacy," I said as I

looked over at the old man who just winked back at me.

"Look, Craig, we are worried about you. What you have been dealing with over the last couple of years surely has taken its toll on you, we just want to help."

I sat on the bed and put my head in my hands and cried. I hadn't sobbed like that for years; I was an emotional wreck. Life had broken me. I just sat and sobbed.

The nurse pulled the curtain back around the bed again and the other woman pulled a chair up and sat in front of me. "Hello, Craig. Before your mind starts racing I'm only here to help you. My name is Tracy and I work for the social services." She put her hand on my back and rubbed it. "You're OK, son. We will look after you."

I lifted my head and rubbed my tears away. I tried to smile but it just wasn't there. I sighed and took a deep breath.

"Look, Craig, you aren't going back on the streets. We are going to get you into a home where other young fellas have experienced the same troubles. You don't need to worry about where your next meal is coming from or where you're going to put your head down. It's going to be OK, son, so stop crying."

"Thanks," I said through my sobs.

"I am going to return in the morning. I will bring you a change of clothes and then when you get discharged I will take you to your new home."

The policeman then said, "Look, son, stop worrying about where you have been, just concentrate on where you are going to be. It's a new start for you – a safe start."

I think he knew what I had been through and felt sorry for me but I still couldn't tell him what I had done. I was relieved when they left.

After they had gone the old man chirped up again. "So you're staying again then, son?"

"Looks like it, for tonight anyway."

"That's good, son. Look, for what it's worth the boys' homes aren't so bad. At least it's somewhere to get your head down."

"Aye, suppose so," I replied and got up and went to the toilet.

The next day around 11am Tracy came back. "Good morning, Craig. How are you today?"

"Better than I was. My leg is still sore but apart from that I'm OK."

"That's good. So are you ready for a new start?"

"Yeah, I am," I replied as she handed me a bag of clothes.

"They aren't designer but I think they are your size." She smiled.

Designer? I thought. *What's that?*

I smiled back and took the clothes out.

"I will give you a bit of privacy to get changed, Craig. I will go and ask when you're getting discharged."

"OK, thanks."

She pulled the curtain around and walked out.

I put the grey tracksuit bottoms on first; they were super comfy. I then put my socks on but could only get one trainer on as my foot was bandaged up and along with the sock over it the trainer wouldn't fit. There was a t-shirt and then a grey hoodie which smelt lovely and clean. I put the trainer back in the bag and sat back down on the bed to wait for Tracy to return.

A few minutes passed and the curtain was pulled back by the nurse who was carrying a brown file. Tracy was with her.

"Right, Craig, let's get you out of here," the nurse said.

I smiled at Tracy who smiled back.

"We will have to get you a set of crutches to help with your walking until that foot heals up but apart from that you are good to go." She handed me a paper bag with a couple of small boxes in it. "These are antibiotics and painkillers. It tells you on the box how many to take and how often."

I looked at her, bemused.

"What is wrong, Craig?" Tracy asked.

"I can't read," I replied, embarrassed.

"Don't worry, I will tell you what you need to take," Tracy replied in an understanding voice.

"Right, so we are all set, just give me five minutes or so to get them crutches for you," the nurse said and left.

"Listen, Craig, this is probably a lot to take in but small steps at a time, that's all you need to do."

"I'm hardly going to burst into a sprint," I joked.

Tracy laughed. "That's not what I meant, it's about starting again, a new life."

"Oh, right." I laughed.

When the nurse came back she gave me a set of crutches. She gave me a few pointers but really they were self-explanatory, or so I thought.

I stood up and got the whole hop thing wrong and ended up on my backside on the floor. The old man gave a hearty laugh out and the nurse just gave him a look that would kill him. She helped me back onto my feet and said, "It's not as easy as you think, Craig, you just need a bit of practice."

My face was beaming. "Them floors must be slippy," I said, a bit embarrassed.

The old man chirped up. "Aye, they are a skating rink." He laughed again.

"Mr. Johnston, that's enough," the nurse grunted at him.

"You have made my day, son. That was the funniest thing I have seen in a while."

"Glad you enjoyed it." I looked over and laughed.

"Good luck, son, whatever or wherever you end up."

"Thanks," I replied and had another go with the crutches.

"There you go, you have the hang of it now," Tracy said. "I will lift your stuff and let's get you out of here."

By the time I got to Tracy's car I was a total expert with the crutches.

CHAPTER 9

LOCKED IN

We must have been driving for a good hour and then we pulled up to a set of gates. Tracy put her window down and reached over to a box and pressed the button.

A man's voice sounded. "Hello, can I help you?"

"Hi, it's Tracy from social services. I have a young fella with me to be admitted."

I wasn't sure what that meant but I took it that this was the place I was going to be staying.

"Hello Tracy, come on in."

The gates opened and we drove in. We pulled up in front of a large building; there must have been 50 windows over 2 floors but it was the bars on them that I noticed. That concerned me. Was I going to a prison? "What's with the bars on the windows, Tracy?"

"Don't worry about them. It's just for security, Craig."

I frowned. I wondered, was it to keep people out or to keep us in?

The large black door opened and two men came out to meet us.

The man opened my door. "I take it you are Craig?

I'm Charles. Come, let's get you settled in."

I swung my legs round. Tracy had already got my crutches out of the boot.

"Thanks," I said as I stood up, taking the crutches from her.

Charles helped me up the couple of steps before I entered the house.

It was a large room with a corridor running down each side and a set of stairs of to one side. All the walls were painted white – it reminded me of the hospital that I had just left but this place had carpet on the floor. It was homely looking but it was really quiet; that puzzled me. "Where are all the other boys?"

"Oh, it's feeding time at the zoo. They all will be in the dining room. We will get you booked in then you can go and meet them."

He took me into a room and explained all the do's and don'ts and to be honest, there were a hell of more don'ts than do's.

Tracy said her goodbyes and said she would check in on me in a couple of weeks' time, but that was the last time I saw her.

I was shown to my room which wasn't that big; it had a bed and a wardrobe in it with a single bulb hanging from the centre of the room. There was a single window which I went over to and looked out onto a large yard with high walls around it and with the bars on the windows I felt trapped.

"Shit. What have I got myself into?" I said under my breath.

"What was that, Craig?" Charles asked.

I turned. "Nothing, Charles."

"It's 'Mr. Taylor' to you, boy, or better still just 'sir'. Now come with me to get you something to eat. I'm sure you are hungry?"

I was speechless. I just nodded and followed behind him, one hop after the other. My heart dropped. *What the hell have I come to?* I thought.

We went into a large room; there must have been 20 other boys sitting at tables all talking and when the door closed behind me you could have heard a pin drop. I felt a thousand eyes on me and I noticed a few of the lads nudging each other and whispering to one and other. You could cut the atmosphere with a knife.

"BOYS, this is Craig. Make him feel welcome," Charles grunted out.

I looked round at all the other lads but they all turned away and put their heads down and continued eating.

Charles brought me over to a table where four other boys sat and told me to sit down. I looked at the boys but they didn't even give me eye contact, they just kept their heads down. As I sat down Charles said, "I will bring your lunch over but trust me, this is the first and last time I do as I'm not your waiter."

One of the boys laughed, which was a mistake. Charles hit him with such a slap on the back of the head I even flinched with the crack of it. "Something funny, Jones?"

"No sir, no sir. I'm sorry," the boy said as he rubbed the back of his head.

"You will be, Jones," Charles replied very angrily.

He walked away and over to a service hatch, coming back with a plate of what I could call some type of soup with a round roll and spoon.

"Get that into you, Craig, or you will go hungry."

"Thanks Charles," I replied only to get a smack on the head as well.

"I will only tell you this once more, it's 'sir'."

"Sorry, sir, it won't happen again."

He walked away and out of the room. The boys started talking between themselves again and I made an attempt to eat the soup. It tasted absolutely like crap – really salty with no taste so I broke the roll up and soaked it with soup.

"Eat it all up, mate, or you will be on the end of another slap."

I looked up and it was the lad who Sir had hit. "Thanks, I will," I replied.

"What did you do to be brought here?" the lad asked.

"Nothing, I was living on the streets and then got bit by a dog and ended up in hospital and this is where they brought me."

"Jesus, you have no luck."

"I'm Craig. What are your names?"

"I'm Paul, this is Jim, and moody bollocks over there is Jack."

"Fuck you, Paul, I will knock your head off your shoulders."

"I'm only having a laugh with you. Told you, Craig, moody bollocks."

The boys laughed and so did I.

After our salty soup we were told to go to our

rooms for an hour and then we were allowed to go to the common room where there was a television and it had a pool table. It was a chance to get to know the other lads and it was then I found out this was a young offenders' centre where most of the lads had committed minor crimes and were here for a minimum of 3 months. I wondered why they had put me here but wouldn't dare ask Sir in case I got another slap.

Paul was in for house breaking; Jim had stolen from an electrical store; as for Jack, he was in for an assault on a teacher, and those were the lads I would keep friendly with until I got out.

Dinner wasn't much better than lunch, with lumpy potatoes and burnt offerings of sausages with some sort of vegetable – I couldn't make out what it was. The nicest part of it was the glass of juice that we got to wash it down with, but I suppose it was better than being on the street begging or plundering through bins for something to eat, so I suppose beggars can't be choosers.

It was an hour or so outside in the yard and back to the common room for, again, an hour or so and then to your room where lights out was ten o'clock.

It was this time I had to reflect on where I had been and what had happened in my life, with some dark disturbing memories, but what I didn't realise was that memories were going to be made here.

Life was just routine here; everything was set for us. The time you got up, the time you had to get washed, the time you ate and the time you spent with the other boys, and of course, the time you went to bed, and it was this time I learned was the most dangerous.

Sometimes at night I could hear a lad crying and pleading with someone. At first I thought he was having nightmares but learned otherwise,

It was a Friday night about thirty minutes after lights out when I heard footsteps outside my door and then the door opened I sat up to see a man in a suit standing the doorway. "I take it you're Craig?"

"Yes, why? Who is asking?"

"It's OK, son. I'm not here to hurt you. I just want to talk to you." The man came into my room and closed the door behind him.

My heart raced. It brought flashbacks of Joe coming into my room at night and taking Cat or making me touch him. I didn't like it, it frightened me. I jumped out of bed. "Get the fuck away from me!" I shouted.

"Calm down, son. I'm only here to talk."

"Get out. Get out!"

The door opened again and Charles stood there. "Shut your mouth, boy, and you do what this man wants or God help me I will lay into you."

I was quiet instantly and sat back down on my bed. The man walked over and sat beside me. He put his hand on my leg. "I have been told you haven't any family, is that right?"

I nodded and dropped my head. Charles left, closing the door behind him.

"Lift your head. I told you I only want to talk." He put his finger on the base of my chin, lifting my head. "That's better," he said softly.

I looked at him. He was about fifty-odd years old, clean shaven with grey hair. I sighed, blinking slowly. I felt helpless and trapped.

"Craig, tell me about yourself. How old are you?"

"I'm fifteen."

"Now that wasn't hard, was it?"

"I could be a friend to you, Craig, if you want, and bring you some nice stuff. Maybe clothes or some crisps and chocolate, if you want?"

"And what would you want in return?" I said cheekily.

"Nothing, Craig, just to come and talk with you."

"Well if that's all it is then yeah, that would be OK."

"OK then. I will call in and see you next week some time and bring you something nice." He squeezed my thigh slightly and stood up. "Till next week then." He walked out of my room, closing the door behind him.

I climbed back into bed but didn't sleep a wink that night. It puzzled me, who the hell this well-dressed man was and why he was allowed into my room and most of all, what did he want with me???

CHAPTER 10

A NIGHT OUT ON THE TOWN

The next morning I went for breakfast, sat at the usual table with the lads I was now spending most of my free time with.

I gave a big yawn.

"Not much sleep last night, Craig?" Paul asked.

The other boys sort of sniggered but kept their heads down.

"No, not really, some man came into my room."

"We know, all the new boys get a visit from him, we have all been there."

"What is all that about?" I asked nervously, not sure if I wanted to know the answer.

"Look, Craig, he won't touch you, he's not into boys, but he will buy you whatever you want just to spend time and talk, so it's up to you if you want to talk to him."

"Bleed him dry, Craig," Jack said.

Jack never spoke much so when he did everyone listened.

"I got all new gear off him so fill your boots, son." Jack put his head down and continued shovelling his breakfast into his mouth.

"RIGHT, BOYS, AWAY YOUS GO!" Charles

raised his voice at us.

In turn we all put our bowls into the baskets to be washed, which was my job in here now. It usually took me and the other lad about half an hour to get done.

After I got my chores finished I went out into the yard for a kick about with the other lads. It really was like a prison; absolutely nothing to do but put the time in as best you could.

It was over a week until the man returned. It was a Saturday evening, around 10pm, I think.

"I don't think we had the pleasure the last time, Craig. I'm Philip," he said as he outstretched his hand. I shook his hand as he sat down on my bed.

"Would you like to get out of here tonight, just for an hour or so to get something nice to eat?"

Bloody right, I thought.

"Am I allowed to go out?"

"Yes, yes, I have already said to Charles, as long as we are back before 12.30."

"Then why not?" I said. As I got out of bed and put my tracksuit on I noticed that Philip just stood and watched me get dressed. It felt really uncomfortable but just I got on with it.

As I walked out of the front door even the air smelt different; it was really nice to get out of this place even if it was only for a couple of hours.

We got fish and chips and sat in his car while I ate it. Philip didn't speak much, he just let me enjoy it.

I scrunched up the paper and got out of the car and put it into a bin which was just opposite where Philip had parked. For a split moment I thought about doing a runner but decided to see what else I could get him to buy me.

As I got back into his car he started the engine and said, "Did you enjoy that, Craig?"

"It was the ticket, really hit the spot, thank you."

"You're welcome, son. I told you before, I could be a good friend to you." He spoke really softly – at times I had to strain my ears to make him out.

We drove into Liverpool city and with it being a Saturday night it was buzzing; the streets were packed with people out drinking and partying. It brought back memories of living on the streets and how I hated Saturday nights as one time I was lying sleeping in a doorway and two boys decided to use me as a football, which left me battered and bruised, so the life I had now wasn't too bad.

"Would you like to go for a beer, Craig?"

My eyes widened. "Yes, I would love to."

"I know a club that won't ask any questions. We will go there." All of a sudden Philip drove a little bit faster. He reached over and turned the radio on and then squeezed my thigh. "Good boy," he said.

It only took about five minutes and we pulled up in front of this really posh-looking club; it had two men on the door dressed in suits with dickie bows. They were both really big and really hard looking. "Come, Craig, let's get a drink." Philip got out and I followed.

As I walked up to the two men one of them said, "Good evening, sir." As the other one opened the door, Philip handed him something. He did it in a way that he thought I didn't see but I saw alright, it was a roll of money, but I didn't let on that I had noticed, I just thought to myself, *This man must be rich*.

We walked through another set of doors and into the bar. It was really posh. I noticed the bar; it was brightly lit and had dozens and dozens of bottles all regimentally hanging side by side and then there must have been ten different types of beer to choose from. "What would you like to drink, Craig?"

"Just a beer please," I replied.

"Go and sit down over there. I want to introduce you to a friend." He pointed over to a booth which I noticed had a sign on it saying 'reserved'. I went over and sat down.

As I sat there I looked around the bar. I began to notice that there were a few other older gentlemen, all sitting with younger lads, and then I realised what this place was. I was just about to get up and run when Philip came over with two pints. As he set the pints on the table he said, "Craig, this is John." As I looked over his shoulder there stood another well-dressed gentleman behind him. He was holding a glass of wine. Philip sat down beside me and the other man sat on the other side of me. I had no way out so I lifted my pint and took a great big gulp of it. It tasted funny but I took another big drink.

"Slow down, son, there is more of that where that came from," John said in a soft, polite voice.

I set my pint down and before I could wipe my mouth John had a white handkerchief out and wiped it for me. I sort of flinched backwards a bit but didn't stop him.

"Charles tells me you're an orphan with no family at all, is that right?"

"It is, sir." I lifted my pint and took another drink. It tasted better this time. As I set it down I burped. I covered my mouth and said, "Excuse me."

"I like manners, Craig, they are hard to come by these days. Would you like another?"

I think I'll take these two posh poofs to the cleaners, I thought.

"Yes, please. I'm really thirsty."

John got up and went to the bar. "Well, what do you think of John?" Charles asked.

"Yeah, he's OK."

"Stay on the right side of him, Craig, he is a very important man."

When John returned with my beer he had a smirk on his face and he leant into Philip and whispered something into his ear. Philip just laughed and said, "You're awful, John, just bloody awful."

He sat beside me again but this time he left his hand on my thigh.

"There you go, Craig, enjoy."

I felt really uneasy with his hand now ever so gently rubbing my leg. I tried to move over a bit but Philip was sitting so close I had nowhere to go. I brushed his hand away but straight away he put it back and this time it was getting a bit too high for my liking. I went to stand up but John just applied pressure on my leg to stop me.

"Now, now, Craig. Stop getting nervous. Enjoy your drink. I won't hurt you, in fact I could be a really good friend to you. If you give me what I want I will treat you really well and you will want for nothing."

I didn't know what to say, I just looked at Philip

and he didn't even flinch, he just smiled and lifted his drink.

I lifted my pint and took a really big drink of it, in fact I drank over half of it and set it back down. John's hand was now resting right at the top of my thigh. I looked down as I felt his little finger softly rubbing my dick. I looked up at him and he said, "So you like that, Craig?"

Before I could answer he put 20 pounds into my hand and said, "If you play nice I have more of this to give you."

I looked at the money and wondered how much more he would give me if I just played along, and it wasn't like he was punching me like that awl bastard Joe did when he made me touch him, especially when I didn't do it right.

"How much more?" I answered.

John smiled and as he leant in close to me he whispered, "Oh a lot more, gorgeous, a lot more."

He kissed me on the cheek and then sat back again. I was so embarrassed my face was burning. John leant in.

"Don't be shy, Craig. Nobody in here will bat an eyelid at what goes on. It's a members only club.

I lifted my drink and as I polished it off I thought, *What the hell am I doing? What have I got myself into?* As I went to set the glass down I felt really funny and I must have misjudged the table but I dropped the glass on the floor and really felt dizzy. My head was rocking backwards and forwards and I couldn't really focus on anything, it all was just a blur. I looked at Philip and was trying to talk but nothing was coming out, only slurs. He put his arm around me and the last thing I remember was him saying, "I think it's time we left."

When I opened my eyes I was in my bed back in my room. I thought at first it had all been a dream but then I felt a throbbing pain in my bum hole and I started getting flashbacks. I had images flashing through my mind of what had happened the previous night. I jumped out of bed and just threw up all over the floor. I retched and retched until I had nothing left to throw up.

Tears were streaming down my cheeks and I had an awful taste in my mouth, and then another flashback. I knew then what the taste was. I retched again and again.

Just then my door opened and there stood Charles.

"Too much to drink, Craig?"

As I looked at him I just cried, then sat back down on my bed with my head in my hands and sobbed.

"Here, take these, it will help with the pain."

I lifted my head and Charles handed me two tablets and a glass of water. I put the tablets in my mouth and took a drink of the water.

"Look, Craig, these men that you met are very influential people and if you were to say anything that you shouldn't, you would be in a lot of danger, if you know what I mean."

"They raped me, sir," I said through my tears.

"You aren't the first, son, and you won't be the last. It's best to say nothing. Have you checked your pockets?"

"No, why?"

"Just check them."

Charles turned and walked out, closing the door behind him.

I lifted my tracksuit bottoms off the floor and went into one of the pockets and pulled out a wad of notes. As I unfolded them and started counting there was 100 pounds. My eyes widened. I had stopped crying but the pain in my bum was throbbing so I lay back down in bed and pulled the covers over me. Grasping the 100 pounds, I fell asleep.

I must have been sleeping a good couple of hours.

"Right, get up, you, and clean this mess up."

I opened my eyes and there stood Charles holding a mop and bucket.

I pulled back the blankets and put my feet on the ground. As I stood up Charles grabbed my arm. "How much did you get?" he said as he snatched the money out of my hand. As he let go of me I fell back onto the bed.

"That's mine, sir."

"I think you will find it's ours." He lifted out a 20-pound note and threw it at me.

"That's your cut and the rest is mine. Put it down to expenses." He laughed and as he turned to walk out he said, "Now get this room sorted, boy."

I sat and looked at the twenty-pound note and thought, was this all I was worth? A measly twenty quid? I wouldn't be so stupid next time, I thought, and then the smell of sick hit me. I put my tracksuit bottoms back on, and socks and trainers, threw my t-shirt on and started cleaning the sick up.

When I finished I went to the bathroom and as I stood and pissed I felt a real sharp pain in my bum and a lot of pressure. I quickly turned and dropped my tracksuit bottoms and boxers down and sat on the toilet. I just made it.

I had really bad diarrhoea, I thought. When the pressure and pain subsided I wiped my bum and as I dropped the toilet paper down the toilet I got the fright of my life; the whole toilet was blood red, and I mean the whole toilet. I had never seen so much blood and it was so vivid red, it scared me. I quickly flushed and went to find Charles.

As I walked back up the corridor I looked in each room as I passed but there was no sign of him.

It wasn't until I went into the dining room where I noticed him standing at the big window. He looked over at me and with his index finger he summoned me towards him. As I walked slowly I could hear the other boys whispering but I just focused on Charles. As I got close to him he said, "Philip is calling later in the week for you so you better play nice."

"I need a word in private, sir."

I could hear some of the boys laughing behind me so I turned to see what was funny. The whole room was fixated on me I didn't know what to say. I could just feel my face burn, then one of the lads said, "Have you got your period, bum boy?"

I didn't know what to say but just then I could feel something cold and wet at my bum. I reached back and felt and then looked at my hand and it was blood red. I panicked and ran. As I made it to the door I could hear all the boys laughing and some of them shouting, "Bum boy, bum boy!"

I burst through the door and up the corridor to the sanctuary of my room. I just fell into the bed, crying into the pillow.

It wasn't long until Charles came in. "Don't be worrying about them boys. I have had a word. They won't be bothering you again. Look, Craig, this is life in here and you best make the most of it before you are left behind and they move on to the next boy, so get yourself together, you could get to make a lot of money from this and set yourself up when it's time to leave."

"But sir, it's sore," I said as I sat up and wiped my tears away.

"It will get easier, not just physically but mentally too. It's like this – what other option do you have? Back to the streets?"

"I don't want to go back there, sir."

"Then just get on with it. I have arranged for you to be picked up again on Friday, now go and get a shower and I will put your clothes into the wash. You will feel better after you get fresh clothes on." Charles turned and left me sitting there.

My mind was a mess. I held my head in my hands. The thought of having to meet these men again, knowing what they wanted from me, was a nightmare. I closed my eyes really tightly and just pulled at my hair. I must have sat there a good ten minutes trying to figure out what to do. I came up with nothing; survival was as good as it got.

CHAPTER 11

Glad RAGS AND MAN BAGS

The rest of the week I just kept myself to myself, avoiding most of the lads for most of the time. Charles was right – nobody said a word to me about the previous Sunday which I was relieved about. As Friday rolled around I was getting really worried about what would happen and who I was to meet but it was out of my control and if I refused I would surely be beaten by Charles.

It was around 6pm when I was in the common room with a few of the lads playing pool and for a few moments I had forgotten all about getting picked up. I was down to a black ball fight with Jim who had held the table for about an hour so when I potted the black the other lads cheered as Jim was finally beaten. It was a good feeling having the other lads congratulate me but I think they just did it to annoy Jim and annoy him they did; he slammed the pool cue down hard on the table and walked off in a huff. The other lads all loved it and berated him as he stormed off.

It was all brought to a sudden halt when Charles aggressively pushed open the big doors and ordered me to my room. "Craig, room, now," he said, pointing his finger at me.

I set my cue down on the table and reluctantly

walked out past him. The room went quiet as Charles followed behind me. As I walked down the corridor my heart was racing. This was it, I thought, my head dropped. I got to my room and was surprised to see Philip sitting on my bed. I just stood there. Charles pushed me forward as he closed the door behind him. "Don't be ignorant, Craig, Philip has brought you a present."

Philip stood up. "Hello, Craig, how have you been?"

"OK, sir."

"Less of the formalities, it's Philip. Here, put these on for tonight, you're going out."

He handed me a large bag. I walked over and set it on the bed. As I took the contents out Philip and Charles were talking behind me. I couldn't make out what they were saying but the only part I picked up was Charles saying, "Yes, same arrangement as last time," so I knew then what was going to happen.

I continued on lifting the new gear out; it was a suit with a nice white shirt, new socks and boxers and new shoes. There was also a nice flashy belt. When I put it all on I felt amazing, really dapper, but was quickly brought back down to earth when Charles said, "Now you behave tonight and do whatever Philip tells you."

I reluctantly replied, "I will, sir,"

Philip put his arm around me. "Good boy," he whispered softly into my ear as he ushered me out and into his car.

As we drove through Liverpool city centre I knew exactly where we were going.

To his posh club.

It was the same routine as last time. Philip tipped the bouncers on the way in and brought me over to his reserved table. I gave a sigh as I sat down and Philip went to the bar. I looked across the room to again see young lads accompanied by older gentlemen. It was sickening to see these men paw over the young lads who were just going along with what these men wanted.

Philip returned from the bar with a pint for me and set it down in front.

"A bit of Dutch courage for you, Craig."

"Thanks, Philip, I think I will need it." I lifted it and took a big gulp.

"Look, Craig, the fella I am getting you to meet tonight is a very important client of mine so whatever he wants you to do, just do it as he will pay you very well and if he takes a shine to you he will want to book you again."

I looked at Philip. "I will. When you say a 'client', is this a business?"

"It is a need-to-know basis, Craig, and the finer details you don't need to know. All you need to know is that you will be paid for your services."

"OK, Philip." I took another drink of my beer.

His phone rang and he stood up and left the table as he answered it. I took it that this was the guy I was going to meet.

I watched as he finished the call and put his phone back in his pocket and walked outside; it was only a couple of minutes before he returned with an older gentleman who was casually dressed but you knew looking at him he was loaded. As they got closer to the table Philip introduced him. "Craig, this is Jeffery, a friend of mine. Jeffery, this is Craig, your escort for tonight."

Jeffery put his hand forward. "Nice to meet you, Craig. Aren't you easy on the eyes?"

I stood up and took his hand. "Good to meet you, Jeffery, and thanks."

I thought it was a handshake but wow, did I get that wrong. As Jeffery ushered himself round the table to sit beside me he still held my hand, and his were really soft. I thought to myself, *This guy has never done a hard day's work in his life.*

"What would you like to drink, Jeffery?" Philip asked.

"Oh, I would love some champers, Philip," Jeffery replied in a really feminine voice.

As Philip went to get drinks Jeffery asked me, "Well, Craig, we are in for a good night. Don't be nervous, I won't bite." He leant over and as he kissed me on the cheek he squeezed my leg.

"I'm not nervous but could we get the formalities out of the way first?"

"Formalities? That's a big word for Friday night." He laughed.

"Payment, I mean." I wanted to get my money before Philip came back.

"Now, now, Craig, I have already paid Philip but if you're a good boy there is more for you later."

"Oh, right, that's OK." I knew then that Philip and Charles would get their cut and I would get the bare minimum so I would have to play the game and try and get as much out of him when we were on our own.

Philip came back with the drinks — a bottle of champagne for Jeffery which was in a bucket of ice, and a pint for me.

"I have to go for a while, Jeffery, but just ring me when you want to go back to the hotel."

"We will be fine for now, Philip, won't we Craig?" Jeffery squeezed my leg again.

"Yes, we are OK here." I knew then that Philip wasn't going to drug me like last time so I was happy enough to stay with Jeffery.

"You're such a delight, Craig. Has anyone ever told you that?"

I smiled. I actually didn't mind being in his company; I didn't feel threatened at all.

"That's good, Craig. I will pick you up in an hour or so." Philip left.

As Jeffery poured his champagne he said, "Don't you just love champagne?"

"I have never tasted it before."

"Well, we will just have to change that then, won't we?"

He poured another glass and handed me it. I took a big drink of it, in fact I nearly finished the glass.

"Slow down. Champagne is to be enjoyed, not as a slammer."

It was really sweet and really fizzy which made me burp. I covered my mouth and said, "Excuse me."

He laughed. "The bubbles always get me too." He lifted his glass and sipped it. "Enjoyed, Craig, enjoyed."

After a couple of glasses I felt a bit drunk and I think so did Jeffrey as he was very chatty and to be honest, drawing a bit of attention to us, which I didn't really like. The drunker he got the louder he got but it was when he went into his man bag that my eyes lit up. When he opened his wallet I had never seen as many notes and when he pulled a red one out my eyes went even wider as it was a fifty-pound note. I realised he must have had a couple of grand on him.

He waved his hand in the air and a waiter came straight over. "Another bottle of your finest champagne, my good man."

"Yes sir, not a problem." And he took the fifty-pound note out of Jeffery's hand.

I sat in disbelief at the amount of money he had with him and that's when I hatched my plan to get a few extra quid out of him.

"So what do you work as, Jeffery?" I asked.

"Work? Are you joking me? I don't and never have worked. That's for fools, Craig. Stocks and shares, my young man, that's where I made my money and a bloody great big pile of the stuff, so when I sold my company I retired and have been enjoying the finer things in life now for quite a long time, and intend to enjoy them for a long time yet." He lifted his glass and asked me to lift mine. "Now, chin-chin, to the night ahead, my beautiful boy." We clinked glasses and drank our drinks.

The waiter returned with yet another bottle of champagne and Jeffery's change. "Just keep that, son. I don't like coins – they mark my trousers." He laughed as he set the change back on the waiter's tray.

It wasn't too long after that when Jeffery's phone rang and it was Philip. "Yes Philip, we will just finish our drinkies and see you outside." He put his phone back in his bag and then turned to me. "Drink up, gorgeous, we will take this back to the hotel." As he said that he kissed his finger and placed it on my lips.

We left the club and as we went outside Philip was waiting in his car. We both got in the back.

It was a short drive to the hotel where I was ushered in through a back door.

"It's this way, my lovely," Jeffery said in his soft voice.

I looked back as Philip drove off and I just followed through the door and up a flight of stairs to a room on the first floor. When we got in Jeffery said, "Make yourself comfortable, I need the loo."

I looked around the room as he went to the toilet. It was quite a nice room with nice furniture but it was the size of the bed that amazed me. I had never seen a bed with four posts and curtains hanging around the top of it.

It really was a nice bed.

Jeffery came out of the bathroom only wearing a pair of pants.

"Have you ever tried one of these, Craig?" he said as he handed me a tablet and glass of water.

"No, what is it?"

"Oh, my boy, it will make you stay up all night, if you know what I mean."

To hell with that, stay up all night. When I finish here I want to go home to bed to sleep, I thought.

I put it in my mouth but beneath my tongue and took a drink of water. When he turned his back I spat it out and kicked it under the bed.

"Are you not getting undressed?" he said as he got

on the bed.

I started taking my clothes off.

"Slowly, Craig, slowly. I like to watch."

I lifted my head and looked at him. He was playing with himself and really getting excited. The more clothes I took off the more excited he got but it was when I took my pants off he started yelling, "Fuck, fuck, fuck!" He was clutching his chest and gasping for air. I just stood there in shock as I watched him pass out in front of me. I wondered what the hell was going on. I put my clothes back on again and went over to the bed. I sort of just poked him to see if he would wake up but he didn't even budge. I shoved him a bit harder and nothing.

He was dead.

"Shit. What the hell do I do now?" I said in a panic.

One thought came into my head. *Just get the hell out of here.* But then there was the matter of payment!

I lifted his man bag and took out his wallet. As I opened it the notes practically fell into my pocket. Well, with a little help of my right hand. I set the bag back and left using the back stairs that we came up. As I got out in the alleyway it struck me that if I went back to the home with this amount of cash it definitely would be taken off me so I instead of going right I turned left and went further down the alleyway to find somewhere to hide my money. About 50 yards or so down the dark alleyway it opened up into a bit of waste ground with a couple of empty derelict buildings. This was perfect. I plundered in a pile of rubbish that had been dumped and found an old biscuit tin. I opened it up and poured the contents onto the ground. I lifted my money out and as I counted it into the tin there were 10 50-pound notes and 20 20-pound notes; 900 quid in total – a clean fortune. I kept 5 20-pound notes as I knew that Charles would take his cut when I got home. It wouldn't raise any suspicion about Jeffery dying.

I sealed the tin back up again and walked through one of the buildings. As I got out on the other side there was a wall that looked like it secured this area, preventing anyone getting in. I walked along the wall until I got to the corner and as I pulled on one of the stones it came loose and there was a gap behind it just big enough to hide the tin. I replaced the stone and then lifted a couple of handfuls of dirt and filled the gaps that I had left. I looked around the area and made a note in my head of where I had stashed my money, and then went back down the alleyway to meet Philip who would now be parked outside the hotel waiting on me.

As I got to the street he was waiting in his car. I opened up the door and as I got in Philip asked, "Well, did you have a good night?"

"Yes, it was definitely better than the last time."

"That's good. Jeffery is a good client; he pays well and knows how to treat a boy. He probably will want you again next weekend."

I laughed inside my head and just thought, *He won't be seeing anyone next weekend except the inside of a coffin.* I smiled and replied, "Hope so. He was exhausted when I left. He was fast asleep."

"Very good, Craig. I like it when I match clients up with the right boy."

It wasn't long until I got back to the home and

Charles was standing waiting. I didn't even get to my room before he demanded his cut and, again, I got to keep 20 quid.

Jeffery's name was never mentioned to me again and I never asked about him. Life then just became routine and every now and again I was sent out to do whatever the client wanted. For the most part of it I blanked it out but there was one time that I would never forget until the day I died.

CHAPTER 12

ON THE STREETS AGAIN

The usual pick-up and drop-off to a hotel somewhere in Liverpool centre and a room number to go to. As I knocked on the door a voice inside said, "It's open, just come on in."

I turned the handle, not knowing who I would meet. The room was dimly lit so it was hard to see who was actually there.

"Close the door and lock it."

I walked into the bedroom from where the voice came and as I opened the door I was shocked to see Charles and Philip both standing there.

"Why are you here?" I asked nervously.

"You know why we are here. You have been skimming, Craig, and we want the money back."

"You have got all wrong. I only keep what you let me keep, Charles." I stood there, really worried about what they were going to do with me.

"You're lying. We know it started with Jeffery. You cleaned him out and then you moved on to the next one. You have got a right wee enterprise going on."

"No, NO, you have got it all wrong. Your clients tip me and I thought—"

"Hold on, I will stop you there," Charles said in a forceful voice. "You aren't paid to think, you are just paid to entertain our clients." He took two steps forward and with one punch knocked me out.

When I came round I was tied to the bed naked and face down. I struggled to break free but the rope was too tight around my wrists and ankles.

"Now, now, Craig. Stop struggling. We won't go any further if you tell us were you keep your money."

"The only money I have is back at the home. You can take it, take it all."

"We already have, now are you sure that's all you have?"

"Yes, it is, I'm sure."

That night 6 different men took it in turns to rape me and then I was dumped in an alleyway with just the clothes on my back.

As I opened my eyes I was just glad to be alive. I knew I could never speak about that night to anyone. I got up off the cold, wet ground and tried to get my bearings. I was dizzy and felt really sick; my whole body ached. I walked for a while and came out onto a main road.

I recognised it. I had been driven down it many times so I knew I wasn't far from the city centre and that's where I headed to get my money.

With no coat and it being late November I was bloody freezing and in shock at what had just happened, but the thought of getting my cash kept me going and after a good hour I arrived at the waste ground I had visited many times to deposit my earnings. Over to the ever familiar wall and to the stone that hid my new life. A few wiggles and out it came. I reached in and lifted my tin. As I opened it up I had a warm glow inside but that was quickly extinguished as it was empty. I fell to my knees, dropping the tin and held my head in my hands. "NO!" I shouted. I had been robbed. I had nothing, absolutely nothing.

I stood up and kicked the tin. What was I going to do now? My life was a mess again; it was back to a life on the streets and with being nearly 18 now I couldn't go back into the care system, I was too old. Even if I could, I knew what life that was and anything was better than that.

That night on the streets was the loneliest I had ever felt in my life. I got out of the rain and just sat in a bus shelter all night wondering what I was going to do.

The old life quickly kicked in and the first thing was to find somewhere to use as my home. There were a lot of derelict buildings in Liverpool so it wasn't hard to find a dry one that was away from prying eyes.

After I decided which room I would make my home, I was lucky enough to secure the old door closed tight at night by jamming a builder's plank against the door and a hole in the ground and with a few old sheets and discarded clothes I was able to make a bit of a bed which surprisingly enough was pretty warm at night. Knowing nobody could get, in I slept really well; my new life was very easy to accept and my old life became a distant memory.

Finding food was easy in the city. As long as you knew which restaurants and what time they dumped their unused food you could eat well. The weekends were when you would make some cash either by begging or if you planned well enough you could extract some cash out of a drunk who had passed out and his or her mates had left them. The easiest was in the alleyways when they needed a piss; even if they weren't passed out you could still get a few quid by robbing them. I never liked this method but I needed the money more than they needed to drink it.

I had been on the streets again for nearly a year when one Saturday night I had picked my target to get my weekly pay when it all went wrong.

I waited in the shadows in my usual spot off Lime Street, just around the corner from two popular clubs near kicking out time. I waited and waited. I always got an adrenaline rush while lying in wait for my victim; my heart was thumping but I controlled my breathing. I could hear voices and when I peeked up the alleyway I could see a fella stagger down. He stood not ten feet from me, one hand holding on to the wall and the other trying to unbutton his jeans.

I walked slowly towards him. Standing behind him, I watched as he was taking a piss. I waited.

His piss was running towards me and I watched as it ran past my old trainers. I lifted my head and to my surprise he was now facing me.

"What the fuck do you want?" he asked.

With one punch I knocked him to the ground. I bent down and turned him over and reached into his back pocket to get his wallet. As I stood back up again he groaned and tried to get up, so with one good boot I knocked him down again and as he lay in his own piss, not moving, I took whatever cash he had and dropped his wallet on his back. I was about to leave when I noticed his nice fancy trainers and by the look of them they were about my size. If only I had just left, I would have got away scot free but oh no, I had to take the trainers.

As I got the second trainer off I stood up and there stood in front of me were two police officers. One of them grabbed me and put me to the ground, placing my hands behind my back and handcuffing them. I also was lying in my victim's piss and had my rights read to me. While lying there thinking about what I had just done, there was no excuse. I knew it was wrong but life on the streets is about opportunity and some of my choices were definitely not the right ones.

"We need an ambulance straight away – we have a young male in his early twenties unconscious and he isn't breathing." I watched as the other police man was trying to revive the lad I had just assaulted. The realisation of what I had just done hit me; the possibility that this lad could die.

The officer got off me but told me to stay where I was and not to move. I closed my eyes tight and prayed that I hadn't killed this guy. I said over and over in my head, *Don't die, don't die.*

It seemed so long before an ambulance arrived and it was then that I was pulled to my feet and marched down the alleyway and onto the main street where a crowd had gathered, and as I was forcefully pulled towards an awaiting police van a few of the crowd were shouting in my direction. It was then that one of them ran over and punched me on the back of the head, knocking me to the floor, and shouted, "That was my mate, you scumbag."

All hell broke loose as more and more police arrived to hold back the crowd. I was dragged into the back of the van and I was so thankful when the steel door was slammed shut.

"Get him to the station!" I heard one of the officers shout. As the van pulled away I could hear bottles being smashed on the side of the van.

I was charged with actual bodily harm and robbery and remanded to HM Prison Liverpool which would be my home for the next 2 years, the guy I assaulted did survive but was in intensive care for 3 months as he had suffered a brain injury.

Another chapter in my life was closed and a new one awaited me in the form of time as an inmate in Her Majesty's prison.

CHAPTER 13

EYES WIDE OPEN

"Craig, you will be calling here your home for a minimum of 2 years. It can be easy time or the hardest time you will ever spend, it's really up to you. All I can say, is that this can be a big opportunity for a young lad to make something out of himself, but again, you will only get out of it what you put in. The only thing you need to remember in here is to do what the guards tell you and don't make any waves. I am Mr. Briggs, the governor of this facility, and I will oversee your stay with us. I will only see you if we have any problems so hopefully you keep your nose clean and we don't meet again until your time is up. Officer Smith will get you booked in and kitted out; he will take you onto the wing which you have been allocated to. That will be all."

"Thanks, sir," I replied and got up from his desk and followed Officer Smith from the governor's office.

He took me to a reception where I had to give my details.

"Name?" the officer behind the security glass said.

"Craig James Andrews," I replied.

"Any medical issues?"

"No, sir, fighting fit," I replied with a smirk.

"That's the attitude that got you in here, boy," the officer replied as he tilted his glasses to look at me.

"Sorry," I replied and quickly removed the smirk from my face.

"That's all I need for now. Officer Smith here will take you and get you your kit. You better look after it as it won't be replaced so if you lose it then it's tough luck."

"Thanks, sir," I replied. I quickly realised that these officers weren't to be mucked around with.

He then took me to the supply room where I was told to strip off and put on prison-issue clothes which consisted of grey tracksuit bottoms, three t-shirts, a jumper, four pairs of underwear, four pairs of socks and a pair of plimsoles. It was the most clothes I had owned in quite a long time.

My old clothes were put in a box and labelled with the date, name and prison number attached. I had to sign a form which was also attached to the box and then they were put in a store room. I was given a clear plastic bag and inside it was a white sheet, two thin blankets and a hard-as-the-gates-of-hell pillow. I also was given a blue plastic bowl, blue plastic plate, and a plastic cup which had plastic cutlery inside it.

"This is what Officer Green was talking about when he said don't lose your gear. If you lose your cup then you don't drink. Simple as that, Andrews."

I was then taken down to B Wing which was general population, and put into my cell.

As I walked in, there was this huge guy lying on his bed reading a newspaper. He tilted the paper to look at me. I sort of just nodded. He frightened the life out of me; he was really built and looked like an absolute wrecking machine. He didn't even speak, he just carried on reading.

"Yours is the top bunk, Andrews, and this is Bobby, your cellmate for the next couple of years."

Two years, I thought. *This is going to be a bloody long time.* The realisation sank in as I set my stuff on my bed. I gave a sigh and said, "Thanks, sir."

Officer Smith then told me to call him 'boss' from now on and then left.

As I climbed up onto my bunk, Bobby said, "If you are going to make it in here, son, tell that screw nothing. He is the governor's lacky and will get you into more trouble than enough, so keep your head down and mouth shut."

"Thanks, Bobby, I will do," I replied. "I'm Craig."

"Craig, you and me will get on like a house on fire if you behave yourself and no awl funny business. Do you know what I mean, son?"

"Yes Bobby, I do know what you mean and you will get no trouble from me, I promise you that."

"Good, good. Then come on and I will give you the grand tour. Lift your cup and plate, it's feeding time."

We were on the ground floor and as we walked out of our cell I looked up through the cage. I counted five floors and it felt like there was a thousand eyes watching me. Ss Bobby asked me to walk with him he said, "It's just 'cause you are new. Everyone wants to know who you are and what you are in for and especially how long is your bird."

"Bird?" I replied. "What is that?"

"Your time, Craig, they want to know what you are in for so it is up to you what you tell them."

"Oh, right."

"Here is where you get showered but I wouldn't waste much time in there as the water is always bloody freezing and keep your eyes open, son, don't get caught getting showered alone. The leeches would love to get their hands on you."

I looked inside. There was just a row of showers hanging out of a badly tiled wall – it was all open, so no privacy at all.

"If you look over there, that is where you make your phone calls." He pointed over to a wall with two phones attached. "If you need to call anyone you will have to wait in line until one comes free. You will be able to queue after dinner from 6 till 8 and then we are locked down again for the night."

I had nobody on the outside so using them really didn't interest me.

"Right, let's get some lunch."

We went over to a queue where the other inmates were standing in line, all with their cups and plates.

"Who's the new fish, Bobby?" one of them asked.

"His name is Craig. Be gentle, boys, it's his first visit."

A few of them laughed but didn't reply. I think they were afraid of Bobby; then, to be honest, so was I.

As we got to the top of the line I watched as Bobby put his plate out and as it was taken off him he handed his cup over too. When it was given back to him there were sandwiches on it and a banana. His cup was also handed back filled with piping hot water with a tea bag in it.

"Go ahead there, Craig," he said as he ushered me to the front.

We went back to our cell to eat our lunch, which wasn't too bad. The cup of tea was unreal. I hadn't had one of those in… Jesus, I couldn't remember the last time I had a cup of tea.

"That was spot on, Bobby, really hit the spot."

"You are on dishes, son. That's one thing you will get used to bunked up with me, that you are in charge of keeping the place clean and tidy and I will make sure the maggots don't annoy you."

Fair deal, I thought. *Sure, it gives me something to do.*

"Yeah, no problem, Bobby. That seems fair."

"Put them two tea bags with the others. We will get another couple of goes out of them later."

I looked over to a small table and there was a plastic container with two other tea bags in it, so I lifted the bags and set them on top of the others.

"Rotation, Craig, rotation. Put them to the left-hand side. We will use the others first."

"Oh, right, just take a while to get used to."

"Don't you worry, you have plenty of time to get used to everything."

"That I do, Bobby."

I quickly washed our plates and cups in the small sink and left them to dry on the drainer.

"Right, come on and we will see about getting you a job."

Bobby stood up.

"Job?"

"Yep. Do you think you are just going to lie in your scratcher all day? You have to earn your way in here, son."

I was sort of dumbfounded. I didn't know what to think.

I followed him down the cell block to a window with an officer behind a desk.

"Have you anything available for this young lad, Boss?" Bobby asked.

"Let me have a look, Bobby."

The officer opened a large book on his desk. I just stood there looking stupid.

As he flicked over the pages he was running his finger down each one.

"Yep, this will do him, it's domestic for the library and common room, not too challenging."

"That's perfect," Bobby replied. "Where does he go to get started and what time?"

"Take him over to the common room, ask for Officer Evans, he will sort him out."

I followed behind Bobby like a lap dog over to the common room where Officer Evans was on duty.

"Morning, Boss, I have a new fish for you to put to work, can you get him started?"

"That's great, Bobby, glad to have him on board. I certainly could use him. Andrews, isn't it?"

"Yes Boss," I replied.

"After breakfast you will come here and clean the tables, then mop the floor. If anything needs to be put away make sure it goes in its right place, then give the windows a bit of a clean and that will take you up to about 10.30, and that's when you go back to your cell until lunch.''

"Right, OK," I replied with a sigh.

"Then after lunch you have to go to the library where you will arrange all the books in order and again, keep the place clean and tidy. If you get that all done then, again, you head back to your cell for lock-up, that should be around 3. Do you understand that, Andrews?"

"Yes Boss, I do."

"Well, no time like the present. You will find the mop and bucket and any other cleaning products in this store over here."

Officer Evans turned and walked towards a cupboard; I followed.

Lifting out the mop and bucket, he said, "The floor could do with a good going over. It hasn't been mopped in over a week so a wee bit of elbow grease is required."

"Where do I get the hot water from, Boss?"

"If you go to the mess hall they will fill your bucket for you."

"OK, Boss."

"Right, I will leave you to it, Craig," Bobby said as he went back to our cell.

It took me four buckets of clean water and over an hour to get it cleaned but it looked good and as I put my mop and bucket away a buzzer sounded and that was me back to the cell for lock-up until 5pm when we got our dinner.

Prison life was very routine and that's how my life went. I had my eyes opened to life on the inside.

CHAPTER 14

HOT WATER AND SUGAR

Week by week I ringed off my calendar. As long as you kept yourself to yourself life on the inside wasn't too bad. I always tried to stay positive and tried to keep busy. I even was able to take a couple of classes during my free time as I was only needed every other day to clean. I got to go to school and after a few months was able to read and write properly which helped with the nights as I found a passion in reading and with the library at my disposal, I got through quite a few books in my time on the inside.

With only 6 weeks left to serve I was actually starting to get worried about what was in store for me on the outside. I knew I didn't want to go back to my old life; things had changed within me, I wanted more from life than what I had been given.

I had a meeting with the careers officer and he assured me that I would be set up with a job and housing when I completed my sentence, which would help with rehabilitating me back into society. That eased my worry, knowing that I wouldn't be back on the streets and probably back to a life of crime.

As I left his office the buzzer sounded for lock-up and as I made the walk back to my cell I noticed a man standing just outside the common room; he was leaning up against the wall just rocking back and forward. He caught my eye as he was pulling at his long greasy hair and spitting on the floor.

"Right, Joe, back to your cell," one of the guards told him.

My ears pricked up. I looked harder at him. *Surely not,* I thought.

My heart was racing. I watched as Joe got aggressive and pushed the guard. The guard reacted by putting him to the floor in a flash and calling for backup.

I stood there, just numb. Could this be the Joe that was my abusive dad?

"Right, Andrews, nothing to see here, back to your cell."

I just stood still, watching as they dragged Joe away.

"Andrews, cell, now!!" the guard said really aggressively.

It startled me. "Yes Boss," I replied and off I went back to my cell.

As the door was locked behind me Bobby was already in lying on his bed.

"Do you know that guy Joe they just put in isolation, Bobby?"

"Why, Craig?"

"I think I know him. What's he in for?"

"He murdered his wife a few years back so he's going to be in for a bit yet, but stay away from him, he's not right in the head."

I got up on my bunk and just lay there staring at

the flaking paint on the ceiling.

Holy shit, it's Joe, I thought. I smiled at the thought of him getting charged with murder. "Slap it up him," I said.

"Well if you are going to do the crime then do the time," Bobby said.

A couple of days passed and Joe was back on the wing. The more I saw him the angrier I got and all the bad memories came flooding back. There was so many times I wanted to confront him but I didn't; I knew no good would come of it.

Five days before my release and I was getting hot water to mop the floors. I had become friendly with the officer in the mess hall and was able to get the water myself and it was then I took my revenge.

While the officer's back was turned and I was filling my bucket, I lifted a bag of sugar and emptied the contents into the bucket. Quickly, I discarded the empty packet.

"Right, Andrews, away you go."

So I lifted my bucket and off I went to go to work. I had worked out that Joe always went and stood outside the common room straight after breakfast, just rocking like he normally did, and that's when I would get him. As I walked towards him he lifted his head and looked at me; he stared hard.

"You! It was you!" he shouted.

I lifted my bucket and lashed the boiling water round him. He squealed in pain and fell to the floor. I dropped the bucket beside where he fell and took a few steps backwards. The buzzer sounded and guards came running over, pushing me to the side. I watched as Joe screamed and rolled around the floor. One of the guards shouted at me, "What happened, Andrews? What did you do?"

"Nothing, Boss, he grabbed the bucket off me and poured it over himself."

"Get back to your cell, NOW!"

I immediately turned and went back to my cell. Bobby came in straight after me.

"What the fuck did you do, Craig?"

"He's my dad, Bobby. He abused me and my sister. I had to I just had to, for Cat."

"Fuck me, Craig, you are going to get more time for this. You only had five days left. Why? Why the fuck didn't you just leave it?"

"I don't care what time I get. He fucking wrecked my life. I hope he dies."

"Fuck, what did you tell the guards?"

"I told them that he grabbed the bucket and poured it over himself."

"Right, then I will back your story up. I will get a couple other inmates to say they saw it as well. Fuck me, Craig, you did it right, he's burnt from head to toe."

"What happens now?"

"You will be taken down to the governor's office and asked for a statement. Remember to say that I saw what happened and everything will be OK."

"I hope so, Bobby."

We didn't get out until dinner time and all the talk was about Joe. Everyone knew I did it but didn't know why. I just got a few nods and a couple of pats on the back.

The rumours of Joe, that he was a child abuser,

went round the wings and that was one thing that wasn't forgiven on the inside. You were classed as the lowest of the low, so I was sort of in the limelight for the next day or so, but it wasn't until Bobby and three other inmates came forward and corroborated my version of what happened that I was cleared of any charges. I had an inner glow and a permanent smile on my face when I left Briggs' office for the last time.

"Well Craig, two days left. I'm sure you are ready to get out?" Bobby asked.

"Not sure, think I would rather stay in for a while longer."

"Don't talk a load of crap, man." As Bobby stood up in our cell it was the first time I had seen a personal side to him. "Don't get me wrong, Craig, I will be sad to see you leave but you're too young to get caught up in this system. Go and make a life for yourself far away from Liverpool. If it was me I would get on a boat and just leave."

"Where would you go?"

"Anywhere as long as it's far away from here. There must be more to life than this shit."

"You're probably right, Bobby, maybe give it some thought."

As we lay in our bunks just watching some crappy show on our wee portable TV my thoughts were of what life would throw at me on the outside. I dozed off to sleep.

The next two days I spent saying my goodbyes but it was the day I was getting out that was the hardest. Even though Bobby was as hard as steel he was a real gentleman with very high morals so it was hard to imagine not seeing him every day. He was probably the only real friend I had ever had and it took me going to jail to find him, so it was hard to say goodbye.

As I walked behind the guard for the last time I wiped a tear away and when I got my personal belongings back it felt real and I was getting out.

"Well Craig, I hope we don't see you again soon and I hope you got something out of your stay with us."

"I did, sir, and I definitely won't be back."

"That's good, son, good luck with your life on the outside. Did you get all your details about meeting your parole officer?"

"I did, sir."

"That's good, then just sign here and you're good to go."

I signed the paper in front of me and I was ushered out.

CHAPTER 15

NEW STARTS

As I started coming round I coughed and coughed. I threw up as well and gagged for air. I could still hear Cat's words ringing in my ears. I turned the old wooden crate back over and sat on it. I held my head in my hands. I didn't know what to think or what to do, I just kept breathing, it's all I could concentrate on. I slowly opened and closed my eyes. My thoughts were of Cat and the life we had here. I just sat and cried.

After a while I got myself together. If my name wasn't Craig then who the hell was I? And I wasn't from here, I was from Northern Ireland. All these thoughts were going around my head. *What to do I do now?* I thought.

I stood up and walked outside. The house was well alight now and starting to collapse. I watched as the roof caved in and sparks floated away into the sky. Billows of smoke rose up into the heavens. I could hear sirens in the distance and that was my cue to get out of sight.

I quickly ran down the lane and out onto the main road and back to the bus stop. In the town, as I sat on the bus heading back to Liverpool I knew then that I didn't want this life. I wanted more. Maybe Bobby was right, just get on a boat and leave this life behind.

When I got back to my flat I sat with a glass of water thinking of what I had just done and as I took a drink my throat was absolutely aching. I walked over to the old mirror that hung on the wall and looked at my neck where my belt had tightened round it; it was red and sore. I shook my head at the thought of what could have happened. I went to the cupboard below the sink and lifted out some painkillers. I tried to swallow them with the water but it really hurt; it was like swallowing glass but I managed to get them down. I coughed slightly but that also hurt so I just went and lay down on the sofa and dozed off.

I must have slept right through the night. I even managed to miss my shift at work which wouldn't go down too well but I didn't care anymore. I had decided I was going to go to Northern Ireland and start a new life. I just needed to make plans and especially get as much money as I could to give myself a chance to make it.

That evening at work I got a verbal warning for missing my shift but to be honest it went in one ear and out the other. I got my shift over with and after I had breakfast back in the flat I started planning my escape from this life and it began with packing my stuff up, which to be honest only filled a rucksack. I really didn't have much but it didn't annoy me, I was heading for a new beginning. I counted my money and with 130 pounds to my name it was enough to get me on the boat and money for a month's rent over in Belfast.

My last shift on Thursday night and with a bit of good timing I nicked a few necessities that I could take with me that would save me some money for a while.

I was booked onto the 8pm sailing out of Liverpool which would get me in to Belfast the following morning.

I pulled the flat door shut for the last time and put the keys through the letter box. As I was just about to leave the druggie's door opened and out he staggered. It took all my willpower not to thump him; if I did, that would only bring unnecessary attention which I didn't need as it was bad enough that I was breaking my release conditions, never mind the police looking for me for assault.

I jumped on the number 23 bus which took me down to the city centre where I went into a café and had dinner before making the 40-minute walk down to the docks to be on the boat for 7pm.

As I stood on the deck having a cigarette I watched as the boat set sail and slowly left the dock. The smell of diesel was thick in the air. I smiled at the thought of leaving all this behind and excited about a fresh start in Belfast. I stood there for a good 30 minutes and watched as Liverpool was now behind me, and as the night sky became darker a wind started getting up and the sea was getting a bit choppy. With the spray of the ocean now coming up over the side of the rusty railings I decided to go back inside and get myself a seat to relax. I pulled the heavy steel door shut and staggered slightly as the boat was now starting to sway from side to side. I felt a bit queasy at the motion of the ship and the stench of diesel fumes; this wasn't good. The more the night went on the worse the sailing became. People were being sick all over the place. I didn't know what was worse, the smell of diesel or the smell of sick – it was so bad that the floor in the seating area was a river of sick. I went to go outside to get a bit of fresh air but one of the staff told me I wasn't allowed as it wasn't safe and to just sit down. I could hear glasses smashing and tables were now moving across the room – it was terrible. At one stage I thought the bloody boat was going to capsize and we would all drown.

I gained sanctuary in the toilets, locking one of the cubicle doors shut, and as I sat on the toilet seat with my feet firmly pressed against the door and each hand pushing against the walls of the cubicle I was able to ride the crossing out. It was the longest night of my life and it was only when we got into Belfast lough that the boat stopped swaying and I was able to get out onto the deck for some air.

I watched as the sun was just coming up. I could see two big yellow cranes in the distance and I knew I had arrived. It was 15th June, 1975. I was 22 years old.

About another hour and we docked and I watched as the lorries were let off first and sometime later we were asked to make our way off. As I walked through the seating area the place was wrecked and the stench of sick was still thick; you could actually taste it in the air and anyone I passed was still ill looking. I felt sorry for the kids that were there – it must have been hell for them. Some of them were still sobbing. As I walked down the gangplank the air smelt that little bit sweeter. I was glad to get off that boat and what was next for me excited me. I had a new spring in my step and as I walked through a wooden shed-like building a police man stood and watched as we all took it in turn to show our tickets. I was a bit worried when he looked at mine but he just told me to move on. I gave a sigh of relief and as I walked out onto the main road there was a row of black taxis all parked regimentally in a line. The drivers, who were all standing smoking, each in turn dropped their cigarettes, putting them out with the sole of their foot, then walked back to their taxis and waited for a fare.

I hadn't a clue where I was going or what I was going to do so I went up to the first one and asked the guy, "I'm looking for digs. Do you know anywhere cheap?"

"Of course I do. Jump in." He opened the back door and I got in.

As he started his taxi he turned and slid the glass partition open.

"Are you staying long?" he asked in his thick Belfast accent.

"Hopefully for good," I replied.

"Liverpool lad, then, are you a red or a blue?"

"A blue," I replied, knowing he was talking about football. I had got to follow Everton when I was inside with Bobby as that was his team and he told me every bloody fact about the club and every player who had ever graced the pitch at his beloved Goodison Park, and he always talked about the 69-70 season when they won the league.

"Oh, a blue nose, then it's off to the Shankill Road for you, son, you will fit in OK up there. I have a mate who has a wee flat for rent and she is easy paid."

"That's great, thanks very much."

As we drove past a big clock that looked like it was falling down he chirped up again.

"That's the Albert clock. It's bloody sinking, think they are going to try and fix it before it collapses."

I looked hard at it and right enough it was leaning a bit. "Oh right," I replied, bemused.

A few minutes later my tour guide piped up again.

"You don't want to end up in there, son. If you do then it's under the road you go and into to the jail." He pointed out a big grand-looking building. "That's the Crumlin Road court house and over there houses the most dangerous criminals in Ulster, from both sides of the community." He pointed over to a high wall with buildings behind it. "So don't be doing anything stupid or if you do, just don't get caught." He laughed and slid the glass closed again.

A few more turns and we pulled up outside a house in a narrow street. The man got out and went into the house. It wasn't long before he came out and we drove on down the street and turned left. We stopped outside a wee corner shop.

"This is where you will call home. It's not much but for a tenner a week you couldn't knock it."

I looked up above the shop it looked alright. "Who do I pay?"

"Come on into the shop and I will introduce you to Mary; she owns the place."

I followed him in and there behind the counter was a middle-aged woman. "Mary, this is—"

He paused and turned before he could speak I said, "It's James, James Andrews."

"Alright James, I'm Mary. Come on in, son, I won't bite."

"Don't be too sure of that, James, this one is

worth a watch'n.'"

"Pat, you're awful. Don't take any notice of him, he's always winding me up," Mary said, smirking a bit.

"Oh, right. I'm here for the room."

"I know you are, son, but there is a few ground rules before I rent it to you."

"I understand. I won't be any trouble, I promise you that."

"I've heard it all a thousand times so trust me when I tell you, if you step out of line, big Pat here will have you out on the street again."

"Hey, you. I know I have put on a bit of weight but less of the big," Pat said, laughing.

Mary just scowled at him.

"Jesus, son, just do what she asks. I would face a punishment beating before I would face Mary." Again, Pat was laughing.

"No smoking in the flat and definitely no parties. The last lad wrecked the place so I have just got it decorated again and I want to keep it good."

"Yeah, that's no problem. Sure, I don't know anyone here. I just keep myself to myself so you will have no worries there."

"Right, then come on, I will show you the place."

Mary took me outside and around the corner where there was a black door. She put a key in the lock and opened it up. As I followed her up the stairs there was a nice clean smell. She took me into a small living area with a kitchen to one side and a sofa and chair with a sideboard on the other. It was really nice and cosy; there was a small bathroom and a not bad size bedroom with what looked like a new bed and wardrobe with a small bedside table and lamp. Again, it was just perfect. As I followed Mary in and out of each room it felt like home. I was really happy for the first time in such a long time.

Mary turned and before she spoke, I said, "It's lovely, Mary. I really would like to live here."

"You need to pay me your first month's rent up front and then," she paused, "what date's this?" she asked.

"It's the 15th, Mary."

"Right, then we will make it that you pay on the last Friday of each month but you need to give me 60 quid then to take you up to the end of July and then 40 quid each month after that."

I went in to my pocket and lifted out six tenners and handed them to her. "Thanks, Mary. You won't regret this."

"Told you, James, I have heard it all before. I better not regret it. What are you doing for work?"

She threw me a bit when she asked that. "Not sure, do you know any jobs about?"

"I do but it's hard graft, son."

"I'm not frightened of a bit of work. What is it?"

"My brother Sidney is looking for a helper on his coal run but he is finding it hard keeping a helper as nobody likes the heavy lifting."

"What's the money like?" I said inquisitively.

"I think he's paying 30 quid a week but you could talk money with him. He will be here shortly," she said, looking at her watch.

"I'm up for that. Will you give me a shout when he turns up?"

"I will, James," she said as she handed me the keys to the flat. "Sure I will see you later."

"Thanks again, Mary," I replied as she walked back down the narrow stairway, closing the door behind her.

As I stood there on that Wednesday morning looking out of my window over the streets of the Shankill, I smiled. "This really does feel like home."

CHAPTER 16

DIRTY FACES

It had been a long night so 40 winks was called for but my stomach had other ideas. I was really hungry and could murder a cup of tea. I went down to Mary's shop to get a few bits and pieces.

"Do you miss me already, James?" Mary asked as I went into her shop.

I laughed. "I need a few things."

"Oh right, what is it?"

"Just a few groceries."

"You work away, love, if you can't find anything just give me a shout."

Mary's shop wasn't that big but I might as well have been back in the supermarket in Liverpool. It had everything from bread to cleaning products, even a few things that I didn't know what they were. As I lifted what I thought was hamburgers Mary was quick to point out that they were vegetable rolls, but as I looked at them they were just meat patties.

"You take them with a fry, son, along with soda and potato bread."

I turned and asked, "What bread?"

Mary laughed. "I take it you have never tried a good Ulster fry up?"

"A what?" I asked.

"An Ulster fry. Christ, you haven't lived if you've never had an Ulster fry, James."

"No, I haven't, but I'm that hungry I could eat a horse."

"Then it's a fry for you, son. I make our Sid one every Wednesday so if you give me half an hour I will get you one as well."

"You don't have to, Mary, but that would be great."

I got what I needed and headed back up to my flat and waited for Mary to call me for my first experience of an Ulster fry.

She was right when she said half an hour, even though it felt like two days. My hunger had got the better of me and I had to have a couple of biscuits and a cup of tea while I waited.

When I went back down to the shop she brought me out through the back and into a wee kitchen. There stood at the sink was a man washing his hands and face; he was absolutely black with coal dust. He had an awl cap on and as he turned to dry his face and hands he introduced himself.

"I'm Sid and you must be James. Our Mary was telling me you're looking for work?"

"Yes, mister, I am."

"Less of the 'mister'. When you say that I turn around looking for my dad. Just call me Sid."

"Sorry. I am looking for work, Sid."

"Well, if you're not scared of a bit of dirt and heavy lifting then the job's yours. I will start you on 30 a week, if that's OK."

"Yes, Sid, when do you want me to start?"

"After you polish off that fry our Mary has made."

I didn't know what to say, I just stood there with my mouth open.

A few seconds passed.

"Well, do you want the job or not?"

"Yes. Yes, Sid, I do."

He put his hand out; as I shook it he said, "Welcome on board and about you being called James, that doesn't work for me, you're Jimmy from now on. Now get that fry down you and we will get going."

Mary was right. I had never tasted anything like it and it didn't take me long to scoff the lot down and with a hot cup of tea I was ready to face the world.

I was shown the ropes of delivering coal over the next few weeks, how to carry the bag on your shoulders, getting through each one's house without bumping into anything, and opening up the coal sheds without dropping the bag and then tipping it in without pouring it all over someone's yard.

Sid was a slightly built man but he was inhumanely strong; he made lifting bag after bag look easy, he really was a machine. As for me, I struggled but when I eventually got the technique right it was not too bad. The worst thing was you went home every night absolutely stinking from head to foot, so it was a bath every night just to get the dirt off but it was my clothes, they were what you would call rotten. There was no point washing them until the weekend; they were taken off each night and thrown in a box behind the sofa until the next morning when Sid picked me up dead on 8am and I was dropped back home for just after 6pm. It really was hard graft but I got to enjoy it and it paid the bills.

I got to like Fridays the best. Not only were you finished for the weekend but after a few weeks Sid took me out collecting the money and it was then you made a few extra quid, especially when we had a good week. Sid would give me an extra tenner and with a few tips I was doing alright.

We had finished our last call when Sid asked, "Well what's the plans for tonight?"

"Just the usual, Sid, something out of the chippy and a night on the sofa with a couple of beers."

"You're joking me. Are you not out for a pint?"

"No, mate, just a quiet one." I hadn't been out for a beer since coming to the Shankill but I didn't want Sid to know I just sat in every night. He would think I was a loner with no mates.

"You aren't sitting in on a Friday night, it's the bloody weekend. Do you know the pub on the corner of Cambrai Street – the Mountain View?"

"Yeah, I do, I've been in a couple of times." (I hadn't, I hadn't been in any of the bars.)

"Well, when you get home and washed I will meet you in there about 9 and I won't take no for an answer."

I was kind of excited, a night out. "Yeah, alright Sid. I will meet you there."

He dropped me off about 7 and I went straight in and got cleaned up. I grabbed something to eat and left the flat about 10 to 9 to make the short walk down the road and to the Mountain View. As I got closer I was getting a bit apprehensive but excited too.

As I walked through the front doors the place was packed with mostly men and I squashed past each person, apologising as I went. I finally got to the bar. It was awkward and I felt a lot of eyes staring at me.

"Alright mate, what would you like?" the bar man asked.

"Can I… can I have a beer?"

The place went silent and my heart stopped.

I felt a tap on my shoulder. I was frightened to turn round; there was a real eerie feeling about the place now and I didn't like it. I looked round.

"Alright, Jimmy lad, it's your round." It was Sid. I gave a sigh and the men started talking amongst themselves again.

"SID!" I said, relieved. "What would you like?"

Before he could answer the bar man spoke. "Just the usual, Sid?"

"Aye, Billy, and a couple of wee chasers to get the night going."

Sid must have been some kind of celebrity – a lot of the men in the bar tapped him on the back, saying hello as they passed him going to the toilets. I was just glad he knew me and before the night was over so did half the bar. He kept introducing me as his apprentice and it seemed to go down well with everyone I met.

I couldn't remember getting home but when I opened my eyes I was in my bed. I closed my eyes again and just pulled the covers back over my head. I didn't feel too good but I thought I'd had a good night from what I could remember.

I must have dozed off again and when I opened

my eyes I had to make a quick dash to the toilet. I felt ill. I hugged the bowl and retched; anything that was left in my stomach was now looking back up at me from the toilet. I thought I noticed a chunk of chicken floating in the now orangey-coloured water and remembered then I had got a kebab-type thing after the Mountain View. I retched again and the taste in my mouth was absolutely rotten. I really didn't feel too good.

I stood up and lifted some toilet roll and blew my nose. After I dropped it down the toilet and flushed it away, I staggered over to the sink and turned the cold water tap on. I started to brush my teeth but it made me gag. A couple of mouthfuls of water and I rinsed the bad taste away, I then cupped my hands under the cold running water and threw it over my face. This shocked me into life. I did this a few times just to try and ease the throbbing pain in my head. I dried my face and went back into my bedroom to find something to put on. My jeans had sick on them; even my jumper had sick on it, so into the bath they went to get washed later. I really couldn't face it now, it was all I could do just to pour myself a glass of water and keep it down so it was back to bed to try and sleep it off.

A few more hours in bed and I didn't feel too bad. It was nearly 3pm when I eventually got up and attempted a cup of tea and toast. It was a struggle but I managed to keep it down. As I sat there focusing on my cup I heard someone knock on my door. I set my cup down and went to see who it was.

I sort of hid behind the door as I opened it as I only had my undercrackers on; it was Sid and he just walked in.

"Alright, Jimmy, how's the head?"

He just walked on up the stairs. "Come on in, Sid," I said sarcastically.

I closed the door and followed him back up the stairs.

"Jesus, Jimmy, smell in here. Our Mary will beat your bollocks in if she came in to check the place."

"I know, I haven't had a chance to tidy up but I will get it sorted."

"I'm only joking. Come on, get your clothes on, we're going for a cure."

"A what?" I asked.

"A beer, you header. The racing is on and I have a few tips I want to get on."

"Sid, I couldn't take another drink, I'm feeling rough."

"Don't talk crap. A beer is what you need to sort you out, now come on, I won't take no for an answer."

I went into my bedroom and lifted out what clothes I had. My wardrobe really wasn't coming down with anything worth talking about so it was an awl pair of jeans and a shirt that was missing a couple of buttons, but when I put my coat on it wasn't that bad.

We went back down to the Mountain View. The racing had just started when we got there; Sid was a bit annoyed as he had missed the first race and what made it worse was that he was tipped the winner.

"That's a pint you owe me, Jimmy boy, it's your fault I missed that."

A pint? I thought. I couldn't think of anything worse.

"Usual, Sid?" the bar man asked.

"Aye Billy, Boy Wonder here is getting them in."

I looked at the barman and he knew rightly I was dying.

"Feeling rough, Jimmy?" he asked.

"You don't know the half of it, Billy," I replied, breathing heavily.

"Here, get this down, your cure is at the bottom of your second glass."

"I hope so."

I handed him a pound and lifted the two pints, turning to give Sid his.

"Here's your change, Jimmy," I heard Billy from behind me.

As I turned to get my change my head was spinning and off to the toilets I went to be sick.

When I came back into the bar I got a cheer and everyone there was laughing.

"Get this pint down you, Jimmy, I swear it will sort you out." Sid handed me my pint.

I took a deep breath and started drinking it. It was tough going but after two pints and over an hour I was getting my second wind and got the taste of it again and that was me on it. The craic was brilliant and Sid did well with the racing – he backed two winners and made a few quid but what was better, he bought the drinks with his winnings so I was even cheering his horses on. I had a few bets myself but no luck. I would have been better keeping my money in my pocket instead of handing it to Ray the bookie who ran a book and also did a bit of money lending, but the punters just handed the money they had borrowed back to him hoping for a winner.

I rolled home around ten or so with a fish supper but remembered everything about the day this time and even managed not to be sick.

CHAPTER 17

SIGN HERE

Sunday morning and I was up with the birds. A good strong cup of coffee and a cigarette and I was ready to face the day. First thing first, my clothes that needed washing, so I got them gathered together and filled the bath and with a bar of lifebuoy soap and a washboard. I got stuck in and gave them a good going over. The sick on my jeans and jumper was a bit stubborn but a good soaking and scrub and they were as good as new. I found an old clothes horse one of the days out on the coal run down an entry and that's what I used to dry my clothes. I placed it in front of the window so the sun would dry them quicker.

Another cup of coffee and some toast and I was out the door for a walk around Woodvale Park. This part of a Sunday I enjoyed the most, especially the earlier the better as there were not many people out and about. As I strolled around the park the sun was shining down just from over the top of Black Mountain; the Shankill really was a great place to live with such scenery on your doorstep. The sun on my face was just lovely and the many birds in the trees getting on with their daily routine was easy on the ears. I even managed to spot a few squirrels busying about looking for food. I sat on one of the many park benches scattered around, just watching them search around the trees looking for nuts and it really intrigued me as they gathered them, taking them back to their hideouts, getting ready for the winter ahead.

As I sat there other early risers were on their daily walk and as they passed we exchanged a 'good morning' but it was when a dark-haired girl walked past, this was the reason I came to the park at the same time every Sunday. I had noticed her a few times before and she was quite a looker. I think she was about the same age as me and with her long dark hair and skinny waist she grabbed my attention. As she walked past where I was sitting she smiled and I smiled back. My heart missed a beat but I didn't have the courage to speak. I wouldn't know what to say and would probably make a complete idiot out of myself so I just smiled and watched as she walked past and out of the bottom gate and back down the road. I really wanted to follow her but I would probably look like a stalker and she would get the police for me so I lit up another cigarette and just sat on a while longer and then went back home.

The rest of the day was just lying about my flat watching a bit of TV and then getting my stuff ready for work the next morning, so it was early to bed and back to Groundhog Day when Sid came knocking to go and get the lorry loaded for our run.

We had to go to the docks where we lifted the load and it was a day's work on its own, loading the many bags on even before you delivered them. A bacon bap and mug of tea out of the greasy spoon café in the docks before we started the run was like a reward for our first hour's work and by God, it was tasty.

Maggie, who always served us, had it ready every morning bang on 9am and by 9.10 we were away and back over to the Shankill to deliver the many bags we had on. This was the normal routine every morning until Friday when we only had half a load to do as we collected the money late afternoon and early evening.

It was 6.30pm and we only had a few houses left to do when we were approached by two guys wearing balaclavas. It was down at the bottom of Battenburg Street. As it was now late October it was dark and with no working street lights it really was pitch black. I was sitting in the lorry when I noticed them and Sid was just coming out of a house after collecting their coal money. One of them made a grab for him but Sid fought back. I looked on in shock as the other guy punched Sid, knocking him to the ground. It was then I jumped out of the lorry.

"Get your fucking hands off him!" I shouted as I ran over.

One of them turned and took a swing at me, hitting me on the side of the head. It dazed me but I was still standing. I returned blows, hitting him numerous times, knocking him to the ground, and gave him a good boot to the ribs, making sure he wouldn't get up too quick.

I turned my attention to the other one. He was doing his best to grab Sid's money bag, so I grabbed him and pulled him off Sid, who was now in a bit of distress at what was going on. The guy turned and I think he had some sort of knife because when he took a swing at me, and only for getting my arm up to protect myself, he sliced right through my coat jacket and into my forearm. This really pissed me off and I went for him. Punch after punch I hit him, knocking two bells of shit out of him. He squealed for mercy but none was given, I just kept going and when Sid pulled me off him I wasn't sure if I was covered in his blood or my own.

"Fuck's sake, Jimmy, stop, you're going to kill him!" he shouted as he pulled me off.

I struggled to break free from Sid's grasp. I had completely lost it and wanted to finish him off but Sid held on tightly and I watched as the two of them got to their feet.

"You're a dead man, a walking fucking dead man, do you know who we are?" one of them said as he struggled to his feet.

"Sid, let me go, let me do these two now!" I shouted and tried to break free.

"Jimmy, for fuck's sake calm down, they are U.D.A."

"U.D.A? I don't give a fuck, I will still have the two of them."

"We will see you tomorrow. You won't get away with this, you scouse fucker."

I watched on as they limped away holding each other up. My adrenaline came back down again and my breathing went back to normal and it was then I felt the pain in my arm. I grabbed it, holding it tightly to stop the bleeding. "Fuck, that's sore, Sid."

"Get into the lorry, Jimmy. You don't know what you have just done, you should have let them take the money."

"Fuck that. No way, Sid, you work too hard for arseholes like that to just take it."

As we got back into the lorry Sid said, "It's different here on the Shankill, Jimmy. If you get on the wrong side of them it's a lead bullet, son. You really don't know what you've just done. Now give me a look at your arm."

I took my coat off and rolled the arm of my jumper up to reveal about a 6-inch slice up my forearm. "Jesus. That's bad, Jimmy, we will have to get you to the Mater to get that stitched up."

"I will be all right, I just need it cleaned up," I replied as I lifted an awl rag to wipe the blood away, but the more I wiped the more the blood oozed out.

"Maybe you're right, Sid, it doesn't seem to want to stop." I held the rag tight on my arm to try and stem the bleeding.

Sid started the old lorry back up again and we drove up Battenburg Street and over onto Tennent Street and down the Crumlin road where the Mater hospital was. I went straight into A&E where when I showed the receptionist my arm I was taken straight away.

"Oh dear, that's nasty, how did you get this?" the doctor asked as he sprayed fluid on my wound.

"It happened at work, Doctor," I replied, not wanting to tell him the full truth.

"I think you are going to need surgery, son, that looks like it's very deep. We will have to get a scan to see what damage is done so it's a night in here as we can't get you scanned until the morning."

"It isn't that bad, Doctor. Can you not just stitch me up?"

"No, if we did that you might have long-lasting effects." He sounded a bit worried when he told me that.

"But it's not sore anymore. Surely if you just stitched it up it would do rightly."

"That tells me that you have nerve damage so it's definitely a scan in the morning, sir."

I tutted. "Ah, crap. That's the last thing I need."

"You will have to fill in a bit of paperwork and I will get a nurse to dress your wound so it doesn't get infected. I really think we will have to get a surgeon's opinion first thing in the morning. Have you anyone with you who can get you some clean clothes?"

"Yeah, Sid is in the waiting area, he will get me sorted."

"That's good. After we get this dressed you will have to go and tell him to get you a change of clothes."

"That's great, Doctor, thanks very much," I replied.

After a while a nurse came in and cleaned my arm and put a dressing on it, then wrapped it with a bandage.

"Right, that's you sorted for now. I need a few details off you?" she asked in a polite voice.

"Thanks, what do you need to know?"

"Just your personal details."

"Oh, right."

"What's your full name including any middle names?"

"James Craig Andrews."

"What's your date of birth?"

"The 16th November, 1954."

"Oh, a birthday coming up then."

"Yeah, I'm 23 coming."

"And where do you live?"

"39a Broom Street."

"And who is your doctor?"

"I haven't had a chance to register yet. I'm only living here four months."

"I can get you registered with the practice on the Shankill road in case you need your arm redressed."

"That would be great. Thanks very much."

"You're welcome. Right, that's all I need. I believe you are spending the night?"

"Yeah, I am. I need to go and see my boss about getting clean clothes."

"Well I'm finished here so you can go ahead and then tell the receptionist that we have booked you into ward 13, she will give you directions."

"Thanks again for all your help."

"No problem. I hope you get sorted tomorrow."

The nurse opened the door for me and I went out to find Sid.

As I walked into the reception area it was packed but I spotted Sid over by the doors.

"Well, all sorted?" he asked.

"Not really. I have to stay in for the night so is there any chance you could nip up to my flat and get me some clean clothes?"

"Aye, that's no problem. Give me your keys and I won't be too long."

I went into my pocket and got my keys. As I handed them to him I said, "I'm in ward 13, that's where I will be when you come back down."

"Right, OK Jimmy, I won't be long." At that, Sid left.

I went over to the receptionist. "Can you tell me where ward 13 is please?"

She looked up from her desk. "If you follow the yellow line to where it ends you will see a sign for the wards." She pointed to the floor.

I looked down and saw the line. "Thanks very much." I turned and followed the line; it seemed to never end but when it did, right enough there was a sign for ward 13. I pushed open the heavy wooden door and was met by an older nurse dressed in a dark blue uniform.

"Indeed, you can't come in here with all that dirt on you, you will have to wait outside the doors, sir."

"But I am to stay the night, my name is Jimmy Andrews."

"I don't care who you are, you aren't getting onto my ward until you get stripped and washed," she said in a sturdy voice.

"And where do I do that?" I asked, a bit annoyed.

"Over here." She took me by the arm and ushered me into a side room where there was a single shower, a table and chair. "I will get you something else to put on. Were you down the mines, son?"

I laughed. "I deliver coal, Nurse, that's why my clothes are so dirty."

"That explains a lot. I will be back shortly with some soap and a towel, just take a seat." She pointed to the wooden chair at the table.

As she left I went and sat down and started thinking about what had happened earlier and what the guy had said about being in the U.D.A. and that I was a dead man walking. It worried me a bit and I just sat with my head in my hands wondering what the outcome would be.

It wasn't long before the nurse returned. "Here you go. These should fit you, Mr. Andrews, and here is a towel and bar of soap. Give me a shout when you get cleaned up." She also handed me a plastic bag to put over my bandage to keep it from getting wet.

"Thanks," I replied and as she closed the door behind her I got undressed and covered my arm. The water wasn't that warm but I got a quick wash and after I got dried I put what looked like prison-issue clothes on.

I put my dirty clothes into the plastic bag and barefoot, I went out to find the nurse.

"That's a lot better now, Mr. Andrews. Now let's get you into bed and get you some pain relief." She ushered me into a bay which had six beds and all bar one had the curtain pulled round, so I didn't know if any of the others were occupied.

I got into bed which surprisingly was lovely and warm and really comfortable.

"I will be back in a tick with your tablets."

"Thanks again," I replied as she pulled the curtains around my bed and left.

A few minutes passed and she returned, handing me two tablets and a glass of water.

"Take these – they will help with the pain."

I took the small paper cup that held the tablets from her and like a slammer I swallowed them, washing them down with the water which tasted a bit funky.

She took the glass and cup back from me. "I will check on you shortly to make sure you are OK."

"That's great, thanks," I replied as she left, leaving me in my thoughts.

After a while a calmness came over me and I was really relaxed and started feeling a bit tired. I closed my eyes.

"Mr. Andrews, we need to take you for a scan," I heard a voice say and I opened my eyes.

"I was told I was to get it tomorrow morning," I replied, a bit dopey.

"It is the morning, sir, you've been sleeping all night."

"Holy God, I don't remember a thing," I replied, bewildered.

"That's good you had a comfortable night, now let's get you down and get that arm sorted." She helped me out of bed and into a wheelchair and she wheeled me away to get my arm scanned.

It didn't take long at all and the outcome was no lasting damage, so twenty stitches and dressed again and I was all good to go apart from having no clothes to go home in.

When the nurse brought me back to my bed she handed me a bag.

"Your mate left these last night. You were sleeping so he didn't stay. Once you get changed give me a shout and I will discharge you."

"Jesus, I must have been out of it last night. I don't remember a thing." The nurse pulled the curtain and left.

It took me about thirty minutes to walk back up home and when I arrived Sid was waiting on me.

"We have had a bit of bother, Jimmy. Someone

broke into your flat last night probably looking for you and when they didn't find you they wrecked the place."

"Aye, fir fuck's sake, is there much damage?" I said as I walked past Sid and up the stairs to see what they had done. As I went into the living room Sid was right, it was trashed. They had broken the sofa and table, smashed my TV in and emptied what food I had all over the place. The dirty bastards even pissed all over the floor. It was stinking.

"Rotten bastards," I said as I started to lift things off the floor.

"Jimmy, it all needs replacing, there is nothing here worth saving. Come on, we will go down and see our Mary and tell her what has happened."

"Sid, she is going to crack and throw me out."

"She won't, it wasn't your fault, you weren't to know who they were. Once she hears what happened last night she will understand."

"Christ, I hope so, I love my wee flat."

We both went into her shop where she was in her usual spot behind the counter.

"Morning, Jimmy. I heard you had a bit of bother last night?" *She already knows,* I thought.

"Yeah, Mary, I'm really sorry about it."

"You have stepped over the line with that lot, Jimmy, and they won't stop until they get you."

"What am I going to do?" I asked worriedly.

"There is only one way to get this sorted and you will have to ask the U.V.F. for protection," Sid said.

"And how do I do that?"

Sid and Mary looked at each other and then Sid

said, "You will have to join, son."

"And how do I do that?"

"I will be back soon. Just you lock the door of your flat and stay there until I get back."

"OK, Sid."

Sid left and Mary handed me a few bin bags and a brush. "Here, you will need these to clean the place up."

"Thanks Mary, and thanks for not kicking me out."

"No worries, Jimmy. As long as you replace all the broken stuff and clean the place up I'm happy enough."

I went back to my flat, locking the door as best I could behind me.

After a couple of hours I had the flat cleaned up and the broken stuff left out in the entry for the bin men to lift on Monday. Sid returned, a bit worried looking.

"You have to come with me, Jimmy, we have to go down the road and meet a fella about getting you looked after."

"Is everything OK, Sid?"

"Not really, Jimmy, the two guys you hit are claiming you attacked them and they want you done in."

"You're joking me. Sure they tried to rob you."

"They are denying it – they said they were just going out for a drink and you assaulted them."

"Fuck me, so what happens now?"

"We have to go to a meeting and explain what really happened."

"And will they believe us?"

"They will have to but I know how this works and it won't end unless you join up, son."

"Well if that's what's needed then let's go."

We drove down the road and into a side street. As we parked the car Sid pointed to a dark green door. "That's where we have to go, Jimmy."

I followed him.

We went up a flight of stairs and into a room. I was behind Sid as we entered.

There were four men sitting at a table facing us. Two of them had balaclavas on and held guns; the other two just sat staring at me. Behind them were the Union Jack, an Ulster flag and a U.V.F. flag, all draped on the wall. In front of them on the table was a rifle and some paper. As we walked towards them one of them spoke up.

"I take it you're Jimmy?"

"I am," I replied nervously.

"Tell us what happened last night."

I began to tell them about the events of Friday night and when I showed them my arm I think they believed my version of events and to help matters, Sid agreed.

"That's not what the U.D.A. told us and they are looking for retribution."

"I don't care what they say, that's what happened and it's me who wants them two fuckers sorted out."

"Watch your tone, Jimmy, we are here to help, we just want the right facts."

"Sorry," I replied.

"Can you go back out again and give us five

minutes?"

Sid and I left to let them make their decision.

The door opened and one of the guys in the balaclava came out. "That's you. Come back in. Sid, just you stay outside."

I looked at Sid. "Just go ahead, Jimmy, I will wait in the car."

I followed the guy inside and he closed the door behind me.

After about 30 minutes I had joined the U.V.F. and was under their protection so the U.D.A. couldn't touch me without a full-on feud erupting.

CHAPTER 18

MY ANNIE

The next few weeks I just laid low. It was just work and home. I noticed a couple of guys watching us on collection day but Sid assured me we wouldn't be robbed again as he had the full backing of the U.V.F. and if anyone tried it they would be kneecapped. It made me feel a bit safer when out and about. I got to know what bars I could drink in and what bars to avoid. It was strange understanding the rule of law on the Shankill and who you could trust. I started to get to grips with loyalism and what it meant to be a young Protestant growing up in the late 70s in Belfast.

Joining the U.V.F. had its advantages; feeling a certain brotherhood especially around July when most weekends were a sash bash and a lot of drinking and partying took place. It was at one of these afterhours parties I had my eyes opened.

It was the Saturday before the 12th of July and we were having a few beers in the Mountain View when about near closing time my local commander asked me and a few of the other lads to go back to his for a few more drinks.

"Jimmy, me and the boys are heading back to mine if you fancy it?" Blackie was a real hard man and when he asked you, you went. He was probably the man I feared the most; his reputation was that he had done time for murder, rose through the ranks of the U.V.F. through fear, and had a fierce temper with the fists to back it up.

"Yes, Blackie, that would be great," I replied nervously as this was the first time he had asked me back to his.

"Drink up, lads, there is more beer back at mine. Jon boy, you organise the taxis."

Jon was Blackie's right-hand man and was the brains of the outfit. He had links to the P.U.P., the political wing of the U.V.F. who were in a constant struggle to stand up against Sinn Féin and their political tactics of undermining the people on the Shankill.

"No worries, Blackie. Give me five minutes."

In total there were eight of us who went back to his house and drank into the early hours. I think it was then that I was accepted within the company and trusted with certain conversations and plans. It was a big step for me but to be honest, I liked it. I had never had this sort of comradery and it felt like now I was part of something and for the first time had mates.

I think it was around eight-ish when I left and was still pretty drunk but I headed for home. It was a bit of a walk as we were up in Ballysillan, the north of the city. On my way back down the road I had to pass Ardoyne shops which were on the edge of a no-go place for anyone from the Shankill. Ardoyne was a grip and run by the I.R.A. who would have just loved to get a member of the U.V.F. and interrogate and then nut just for the sake of it. So it was head down and a quick step as I passed them and down onto Twaddell Avenue and back to my beloved Shankill Road. I called into the local shop to get a paper and he had hot sausage rolls to feed my hunger.

As I sat in my favourite place (Woodvale Park) eating my breakfast and reading the paper, I smelt a lovely sweet smell. I closed my eyes briefly and took a deep breath through my nose, smelling the beautiful scent. I opened my eyes and raised my head and there walking towards me was the girl I had hoped I would see. I smiled at her and as she looked in my direction she smiled back. I don't know if it was the drink still in my system but I had gained a certain kind of bravery.

"Morning," I said.

She smiled. "Morning," she replied.

I stood up to greet her but forgot about my paper and sausage and rolls which now fell to the ground and with there being a bit of a breeze my paper fell apart and started to blow down the park. She did her best to grab it but to no avail – it was away.

"It's OK, don't worry about it," I said as I brushed the crumbs of the sausage rolls off my top and jeans. She was now standing beside me holding one or two pages of my paper. Our eyes met. She reached out and brushed my cheek slightly.

"You missed a bit."

My heart was racing. I nervously wiped my face. "Thanks," I replied.

"A late night?" she asked.

This was the first I had heard her speak; she had a soft tone to her voice.

"Something like that. I should have gone home

when I had the chance."

"So where is home?"

We were actually having a conversation, something I had wanted for weeks.

"I live above the wee shop in Broom Street, what about you?"

"Just around in Orkney Street off Tennant Street."

"Aye, I know where that, is I have had a pint in Bootle Street club."

"I don't live far from there, a few doors away."

"Can I walk you home?" I really was on a roll now, my confidence was flying.

"Yeah, I would like that, I'm Annie," she replied in her soft voice.

"I'm Jimmy. Nice to finally meet you, Annie."

As we walked back down the Woodvale and onto the Shankill we continued to chat and before we knew it we had reached her street.

"This is my house." She pointed.

"Oh, right, that didn't take long," I said, disappointed.

"Yeah, I was enjoying the chat. Maybe we could meet up later?" Annie asked.

I was in a bit of shock. *She wants to meet me later. Nobody has ever asked that, especially not a beautiful girl like her,* I thought.

"Yeah, I would like that." Just as I answered her front door opened and this wee woman was standing there. "And who is this, Annie?" she asked in a stern voice.

"Mum, this is Jimmy." Annie turned to me. "Jimmy, this is my mum, Lilly."

I out stretched my hand. "Nice to meet you, Lilly."

She didn't put her hand out. It felt awkward; I dropped my hand. "If you're going to be meeting my daughter make sure the next time you do you aren't stinking of drink, Jimmy. Now come, you, get into the house." Lilly and Annie went into the house and closed the door leaving me standing there dumbstruck.

I lifted my hand to cover my mouth and breathed out. As I smelt my breath, Lilly was right, I was absolutely rotten with drink and had let myself down especially in front of Annie. As I turned to walk away I heard a voice from above me. I looked up.

There in the open window was Annie. "Meet me in the park about three, Jimmy." Before I could answer she had the window closed, but I smiled and turned and headed for home.

It really was only round the corner so it didn't take me long, especially now I had a spring in my step.

I did my best to get a few hours' kip but it was useless I was too excited to meet Annie so around one, I got up and made some lunch. I was starting to feel a bit rough with the effects of a night's drinking but was determined it wasn't going to ruin my day, so a shave and a good bath sorted me out. I had to brush my teeth a few times to remove the taste and smell of the beer but by the time 2.30 came around I had a quick cup of coffee and I was off to meet her. I called into the shop on the Woodvale to get her some flowers but they were all out so I had to improvise.

I went into the park and over in one of the corners was a patch of grass that had daffodils growing on it so I lifted a couple of good handfuls and with what probably was one of the pages of my paper from earlier that had ended up in a hedge, I wrapped the flowers and it looked like I had got them in the shop. I was pretty pleased with myself.

As I sat on my favourite bench waiting on Annie I was getting a bit nervous. The drink had long since worn off now and I wasn't as confident as this morning. A few minutes passed and then I noticed her walking through the park. I stood up and began to walk towards her. As we met my heart was beating a lot faster. She was as I remembered – absolutely stunning. She had a wee flowery dress on with a cardigan covering her shoulders and with her long dark hair and blemish-free skin she really was beautiful and I think I had fallen for her. "Hi, Annie, these are for you." I handed her the flowers.

"Thanks very much, Jimmy. They are lovely. Will we go for a walk around the park?"

I would go anywhere with her so the park was good enough. I was just happy to be in her company. "Yeah, that would be nice."

As we walked around the park we got to know each other a bit better. I couldn't have told her about my previous life, in fact I couldn't tell anyone, that part of my life was buried really deep in the back of my head. I just told her I had come to Belfast looking for work and that my parents were still living in Liverpool but I didn't bother with them anymore. She didn't ask too many questions about that so I was glad. I learned that she was an only child and that her dad had passed away a couple of years ago. When I asked how he died she went quiet and I knew she didn't want to speak about him so I didn't push her on it.

After a few laps of the park I offered to take her for a cup of tea in a café on the Woodvale road.

"It's good to get a seat," I said.

"Yeah, Jimmy, my feet are killing me. These heels really aren't made for walking."

I looked down at her shoes. "Yeah, but they look good," I said, laughing slightly.

Annie laughed too.

We sat and enjoyed not just the tea but each other's company. I really did feel comfortable in Annie's company and hoped she felt the same in mine.

When I dropped her home wee Lilly was standing at the front door, waiting. I held my breath as we approached her.

"Mum, these are for you. Jimmy got them for you." Annie handed her mum the flowers. *What a genius move,* I thought.

"Awk, Jimmy, thanks very much, my favourite too. Nice to see you cleaned up."

"Thanks Lilly, you're welcome." I gave a wee wink to Annie; she really was a gem. "Can I see you again, Annie?" I asked.

She leant over and kissed me on the cheek. She whispered, "I would like that."

"Right, you, in for your tea," Lilly said, glaring at me.

I smiled. "Sure, I will call round on Wednesday about 7 if that's OK?"

As Annie turned she had a glint in her eye. "Yeah, Jimmy, see you then."

CHAPTER 19

THE GLORIOUS 12TH

The following Saturday was the 12th of July and with this being my first 12th I didn't know what to expect. Sid had been talking about it for weeks.

I was told to meet in the Mountain View for 7am and was given my orders for the day ahead. I was to walk with one of the local Orange lodges as a marshal to make sure they wouldn't get into any trouble, especially at a flash point at the bottom of Clifton Street where Nationalists would be gathering for a confrontation.

There were four of us to walk within the ranks of the lodge and we were looking forward to the day ahead.

"Jimmy, your round," Daza said. Darren was in my unit as well and was a big drinker.

"No worries, Daza. Four pints, is it?"

"Yeah, Jimmy."

We stayed about an hour having drinks and a couple of bacon baps which went down a treat and then the Master of the lodge asked everyone to form up outside.

The band they had for the day was from Scotland and was a really big band; two rows of side drummers, two bass drummers and 10 rows of flutters. I reckon there would have been 80 of them including the guy on the poll.

The Shankill was absolutely packed with people and as the band marched down the road with the lodge behind them, it was amazing. The people cheered as we walked past and the band was fantastic. I had never heard these tunes before but it gave me goosebumps as the thud of the bass drum echoed in my ears. We walked the whole way down the Shankill and through Shankill estate and out onto the Crumlin road where we met with other lodges and bands. At Clifton Street, we stayed there about 20 minutes and then as we formed up again to march into Belfast city centre to meet up with other districts, that's when it kicked off.

There were crowds of young lads all had gathered opposite a chapel in a Nationalist estate. The police had a few Saracens parked trying to hem them in but there were just to many of them and as we marched past they broke their ranks and attacked us. It was bedlam – bottles, bricks and really anything they could get their hands on was thrown at us and a few bandsmen and lodge members got injured. As for us (the marshals), we got stuck into them. The four of us could handle ourselves. I think that's why Blackie put us with this lodge as they had been attacked the past couple of years. We hammered the heads of as few of them and that got them on the retreat. It maybe only lasted a few minutes but it was really vicious and by the time we got everyone back in the ranks the police didn't know what to do. They did their best but were undermanned against a crowd who were willing to do anything to get at us.

We had a break in Royal Avenue and patched up the wounded. The Master of the Lodge thanked us for our actions and said it probably prevented some of the older members from being injured.

During the day there were no other incidents and I was overwhelmed by the sheer number of people not even watching the parade, but bands and lodges. When we walked up the Lisburn road it was as far as the eye could see, an ocean of red and blue and the constant sound of bands beating out their tunes.

We arrived at a place called Ballinderry where we had a couple of hours' break, that's when the craic was flying as well as a couple of beers and sandwiches. It really was a brilliant day out.

After a few speeches from the orange order we got ready for the walk back home.

We left the field about 5.30pm on a bright Saturday evening. The weather really was glorious; our route took us down Shaw's Bridge onto the Malone road then across to the Lisburn road and down towards Belfast city centre. The crowds were six deep and everyone was in really good form. When we got to Royal Avenue we broke off and left the main parade to head back up the Shankill road. It was when we got to Peter's Hill that again we were met by a huge crowd of Nationalists who were waiting for us to arrive. It probably hyped them up a bit more when the band played the sash; it was then that it all kicked off.

They surged forward, breaking the police line, and started attacking band and lodge members. It was bedlam – fights broke out all over the place. Some of the crowd had batons and other assorted weapons, causing a lot of injuries to elderly lodge members. The four of us could only manage to fight so many of them off but it was useless, they were overpowering us with sheer numbers. It was only when supporters came running to our aid we were able to fight them off. But when I broke free from the grip of two lads and noticed a lone gunman come from an alleyway, it was like time stood still. As I watched him slowly walk forward, pointing his handgun, I don't know what came over me but I took a run at him, wrestling him to the ground. I could hear a woman screaming and someone else shouting, "He has a gun!"

The two of us were in a fight for our lives and we exchanged blows. I grabbed his right hand which held the gun and pulled it in towards his body and then BANG, it went off and I heard a loud scream.

I got up off him and grabbed the gun from him. I took a step back probably in shock at what had just happened.

I watched as the blood oozed from his chest and even though he was wearing a balaclava he gasped for air and it was his eyes, they were wide open and full of fear.

I felt a hand on my shoulder. "Run, Jimmy, fir fuck's sake get out of here." It was Blackie.

I put the gun in the inside pocket of my jacket and took to my heels, running up the road along with everyone else. It was frantic; women and kids screaming, elderly lodge members lying on the road injured, but I knew I couldn't stay and help, I had to get offside.

It was only when I got up past Agnes Street I stopped running. I was really out of breath and could hardly breathe so I sat on a shop window and got my thoughts together along with my breath.

I watched as other people scurried by heading for the safety of their homes, all frightened and probably in shock at what had just happened. The sound of police sirens was in the air and it was when Daza came walking up the road I learned the full extent of what had happened.

"Jimmy, fuck me, you have killed him, what came over you?"

"I don't know, Daza. I just seen the gun and had to do something."

"You're a brave man, Jimmy. You could have been killed."

"I know, mate, but I didn't and that I.R.A. bastard got what he deserved."

"You're right, mate, he did. Now come on, I will get the drinks in and you can get cleaned up."

We walked up the road and into the Mountain View club where the rest of the team were already there.

Blackie was first to come over to me. "Get them clothes off you, son, and give yourself a good wash. Here, put these on you and put your clothes and I mean all your clothes in this bag." He handed me a black bag and told me to go to the toilets to get changed.

As I got undressed, I saw my top and trousers were soaked in the guy's blood. Blackie had given me a full change of clothes and when I got washed and dressed I felt a lot better. I put my clothes into the bag but kept the gun and hid it behind the cistern.

I went back out to the bar which was now packed with fellas. As I walked back over to my team I was treated like a hero and each fella I passed patted me on the back telling me well done.

"Get this down you, Jimmy. I'm sure you're in shock, son." Blackie handed me a whiskey and I downed it in one. It was warm as it travelled down my throat and it relaxed me. I was handed a pint and Blackie said, "No money is needed in here again, Jimmy. You did an extremely brave thing today. That gunman was out to murder anyone that crossed his path and you stopped him. I want you to be my personal minder from now on and you will never have to put your hand in your pocket again. You saved lives today, Jimmy, and it won't be forgotten."

I was overwhelmed with pride. "Thanks, Blackie, that means a lot but I would rather pay my way. I don't like freebees."

"Well tonight is on me, then. You're a strange man, Jimmy, but I would rather have you with me than against me." He patted me on the back and I knew then that I had moved up the ladder a bit.

My clothes were taken away and disposed of and Blackie gave me 100 quid to get them replaced. I tried to refuse the money but he insisted so I didn't turn it down.

I was off work for a week's holiday and spent as much time as I could with Annie. I had fallen for this girl and she for me; we were madly in love and even spent a night in my flat which was amazing. Over the next couple of months we were inseparable. I even didn't spend as much time in the club, which was a big thing for me. I only went when Blackie needed me there and shadowed him when he needed to across to East Belfast for meetings.

CHAPTER 20

BAD NERVES

Life was really good. Everything was going well with Annie, work was a gift and the money was good. I had gained a lot of respect from my team and was the talk of the road for a while. I would rather have stayed in the shadows but the attention was good.

One Saturday afternoon I nipped into the club for a couple of pints before I was to meet Annie but the main reason was to retrieve the gun and put it somewhere safe so that no one would ever find it, and I knew the exact place that would be.

"Alright, lads, that's me away. I will see yous during the week."

"Dead on, Jimmy, enjoy your night."

"I will, Daza, thanks." I left the club and headed for Annie's. I was a wee bit early but I had my reasons. As I stood knocking on Annie's front door, wee Lilly answered.

"Come on in, Jimmy, she won't be a minute."

"Thanks, Lilly." As I followed her in I asked, "Is it OK if I use your toilet?"

"Yes, son, work away, you know where it is."

I walked on out to the kitchen and out of the back

door and into the small yard where the toilet was. As I opened up the old wooden door I reached for the light and pulled the cord. I closed the door behind me and reached up, pushing the wooden board to one side, as I went to place my gun up out of sight I felt something cold and hard. I lifted it down. It was an old tin box that looked like it had been there for a while as it was rusty. I set it on the toilet seat and opened it up; inside was a tattered piece of paper and an old photo. I didn't have time to look closer as Annie called me, so I put the gun into the tin along with the paper and photo and placed it back in the ceiling of the toilet. Replacing the board, I flushed the toilet and left. Annie was waiting for me in the front room.

"Hi, gorgeous, how's you?" I asked.

"I'm OK, what about you?" She seemed not herself.

"Looking forward to a couple of beers. I believe this singer is good that is on tonight." We were going just across the road to Bootle Street for a night out.

The night was going OK. Annie was really quiet, though, she wasn't even having a drink, she only had a Coke.

"What's wrong, love? You are very quiet tonight," I asked.

"Nothing, Jimmy, just not feeling it tonight."

"Do you want to go and get some chips?"

"Yeah, I would like that."

We finished our drinks and left. As we walked up Tennant Street to the chippy she held my hand that little bit tighter.

"Jimmy, I don't know how to tell you this but I

have to."

"Jesus, Annie, this sounds serious."

"It is, Jimmy." She started crying.

I put my arms around her. "What's wrong, love?"

She lifted her head from my chest and wiped a tear from her cheek. "Jimmy, I'm pregnant."

"You're what?" I asked, in shock.

"I'm pregnant," she repeated with tears now flowing down her cheeks.

"Jesus, Annie, that's fantastic! Oh my god, I'm going to be a dad and you mum." I threw my arms around her. "I love you, Annie, and will love this wee baby even more."

I was so chuffed.

"What are we going to do, Jimmy? My ma will kill me when she finds out and what will the neighbours think?" She genuinely was upset and all over the place. Her emotions had her in bits.

"If that's all you're worried about then there is only one thing left to say."

I got down on one knee in the middle of Tennent's Street. "Annie, would you marry me?"

She took my hand and pulled me to my feet. As she threw her arms around me (still crying uncontrollably), "Yes, Jimmy, I would."

We stood and hugged for a few minutes and then exchanged a kiss. She couldn't have made me happier.

"What do we do now, Jimmy?"

"We get married. I will see Daza. He owes me one so he will get the details sorted for us, but we will have to tell your mum first."

"I couldn't tell her I'm pregnant, she will still flip."

"No, we will tell her after we get married, she doesn't need to know."

"Yeah, I think that's best but it will have to be soon as I'm already about six weeks."

"I will see Daza tomorrow and see what he can do, now let's go and tell your mum."

Wee Lilly took it well. She was chuffed to bits for the two of us; her only concern was where we would live but I assured her I would find somewhere for us and it definitely wouldn't be my flat so she was as happy as we were.

Annie stayed over in my flat and we just lay in bed cuddling most of the night. I was so happy and for the first time in my life felt alive and was so in love.

I dropped Annie home after breakfast and went to meet Daza to get the wedding plans in place. He said he would make a few phone calls during the week and get it sorted for us.

At work on Monday I told Sid about my good news and swore him to secrecy about the baby. He was so happy for us and told me he would ask around to see if there were any wee houses going that would suit us. Living here and away from Liverpool was the best thing ever to happen to me. My dark past was now just a memory and at times I thought it had to be a dream; it didn't seem real compared to the life I now had.

Daza got us a date in city hall to get married. It was only four weeks away but we booked. It didn't give us much time to get things organised but with the help of Sid and Daza we were able to get upstairs in the Mountain View and got outside caterers for food. We also got a singer booked for a couple of hours to finish the night.

As for the housing situation, Sid had a friend, a housing executive, who was able to get us a wee house up the street from my flat which would suit us down to the ground. It was a two-bedroom mid-terraced house with a small back yard, something similar to Annie's but our bathroom was inside and up the stairs so it was just perfect for us, and better still it was ready to move into. We just needed a few more bits of furniture and that would make it a home. Sid was brilliant and to be fair, Daza sorted the money things out. He told me it was the least he could do and it would be his gift to us for a wedding present,. I couldn't tell Annie the U.V.F. was paying for everything, she wouldn't have gone ahead with it. I just let her believe I had borrowed the money and would pay it back weekly. I think the less she knew about it, the better, and any time she asked I would just tell her it was sorted.

The next three weeks flew by and it was the day of our wedding. Saturday 9th October 1976 was the day I married my Annie. The ceremony was short and sweet; we only had a few people at city hall which was a grand building and the room we were married in was absolutely beautiful. It really took my breath away; well, nearly, it was Annie that took my breath away. She was stunning and made me so proud to call her my wife.

We had a few photos taken outside in the grounds and then Daza had organised a couple of black taxis that were decorated with nice pink ribbons to take us up to the Mountain View where everyone was waiting for a party. And party we did. After we got the speeches out of the way the drink was flying; we had a nice meal and then the singer came on which went down a treat. It even ended up a bit of a sash bash with a few loyalist tunes thrown in.

We wrapped it up about one or so and went home to our house in Broom Street. It had been a long stressful day for both of us and we fell into bed exhausted.

My life was just perfect. Work was going well, Annie and I were madly in love and we couldn't wait for our wee baby to come.

A few weeks passed. One wet miserable Monday out on the coal run we had just got to our first drop off when I jumped out of the lorry to lift a bag of household and slipped on the wet surface and hit the road hard. I got up as quick as I went down but something wasn't right. My back went into a spasm and I fell back to the ground in excruciating pain. Sid at first thought it was funny but when he heard my screams he knew it wasn't normal and came to my aid.

"Jimmy, what have you done?"

"Christ, Sid, my back is away. I can't get up."

The rain was now pelting down and I was soaking wet.

"Come on, Jimmy. I will help you up."

Sid bent down and tried to lift me up but it was no use, I couldn't move. The pain was horrible; it was going up and down my both legs and my lower back was in such agony that I couldn't move anywhere.

"We will have to get you an ambulance, Jimmy, this isn't right."

I winced in pain again and I felt really sick. Tears free flowed down my cheeks and I tried my best not to be sick. Sid went to the nearest house and phoned for an ambulance which arrived a short time after.

"Oh, dear. What has happened, sir?" the ambulance guy asked.

"He slipped and fell and hasn't been able to get up," Sid explained.

I was freezing cold and soaked right through. I wasn't sure if it was how cold I was or the pain I was in but I couldn't stop shaking, which didn't help with the pain, it made it worse.

"We will have to take you to hospital, sir, to get you checked over, but let's give you something for the pain."

He put a mask over my face and asked me to try and breathe normally. At first it tasted funny but it really did help with my back. As the pain subsided I was able to get onto the stretcher and the two guys lifted me into the back of the ambulance. My head was spinning; this stuff was great but it made me feel really sick and sick I was, all over myself, and by the time they got me to the hospital I was in a mess.

I spent the next three days getting bloods done and had my back scanned twice as the first scan wasn't conclusive, but the second one revealed I had severely damaged two discs in my lower back and in turn had damaged the nerves. The doctor told me that I needed surgery but it wasn't a guarantee and had a 50/50 chance of success, and if it didn't go well I could end up paralysed and spend the rest of my life in a wheelchair.

I lay in bed for a while just listening to what the doctor was telling me. It didn't seem real and then I heard him say, "Have you any questions, Mr. Andrews?"

"So what happens if I don't get the operation?"

"You still will have mobility but it will be a case of pain control and it would be my recommendation that this is the route we will take. Look, Mr. Andrews, if I was in your shoes I would take the latter of the options. We could definitely manage your pain but you most likely will not work again as your mobility will be limited."

"I understand, Doctor, so what happens next?"

"We will organise some physio to see if we can manipulate the discs back to where they should be which will hopefully get you up and walking again and then it will be medication for the nerve damage. We will get this done sooner rather than later to try and stop any more damage."

"That's great, Doctor, thanks very much."

I lay in that bed, numb, not just physically but mentally too, and wondered what my future would now be.

CHAPTER 21

BOOTS AND BARS

My working life as a coal man was over; there was no chance of lifting the 50kg bags anymore. I had to sign on and with my medical records I was able to get disability living allowance, or the D.L.A. for short, so money wasn't going to be what I was used to earning and with our baby on the way I had to earn money in other ways, and that's where Daza came in.

I was given more responsibility with in the U.V.F. as a debt collector and with my reputation on the road I never had any grief and nobody was ever late with their payments. It paid well and didn't interfere with my D.L.A. I couldn't tell Annie what I did for the U.V.F. She wouldn't have agreed with it so it was my secret to keep along with all my other secrets from my past.

My problem with my back was always going to cause me issues but with medication I was able to control the spasms, which were now down to once a week or so and when they happened I could only go to my bed for a day and take my meds to relieve the pain and wait for the spasm to pass.

Annie and I had to attend the hospital for a scan and when I saw this wee baby in her belly and when I heard its heart beat I was overwhelmed with love and joy. It was totally amazing that we were to be parents in just a few months.

"Well Jimmy, what did you think of our wee baby?"

"I have never felt such love before that I do now. It's fantastic, love."

"I know, that's how I feel too, it makes it more real now we are at twenty weeks and you can see its wee face and how amazing was it when he waved his wee hand?"

"Hold on, you said he."

"Were you not listening to the nurse?"

"No, I was just watching the screen and listening to its heart beat. So we are having a boy?"

"Yes, Jimmy, you're having a boy."

"That's fantastic, Annie, that's just bloody fantastic." I was overjoyed. I was going to have a son.

When we got back home I went out to celebrate the news with a few pints. Well, to be honest it was more than a few. I ended up rolling home after 1am blind drunk but I had good reasons. I was celebrating.

"What bloody time do you call this? And look at the state of you, Jimmy."

"I know, love. I'm sorry but the boys kept me out," I slurred.

"Just you stay on the settee. You aren't in any state to go up the stairs."

"OK, love." I staggered over to the settee and slumped onto it. Annie put a blanket over me and that's where I slept.

The next day was all picture and no sound. I think

I overdid it with the beer and felt a bit rough so by lunchtime Annie left to go to her mum's and I sneakily went for a cure before I did a bit of debt collecting, which was a struggle, and my hangover got the better of me. So it was back to the club for another couple of pints to sort me out and call in for chips and a hasty return home before Annie got back. I got the tea pot on and bread buttered just as she came in through the front door.

"Hi, love, how's your mum?"

"So you've sobered up then?"

"Course I have. It was a one-off, love. I was just chuffed at the news of our wee son."

"I hope it was a one-off, Jimmy, you have responsibilities now and I don't want a drunk of a dad for our boy."

"I don't either, love. It won't happen again, I promise you that. I got us a fish supper for tea so I hope you are hungry?" I said in the hope she would forgive me.

"Yeah, I'm famished. I hope you got extra vinegar on them."

"Yes, just the way you like them." It looked like I was in the clear.

We sat and ate our dinner and washed the chips down with a big mug of strong tea.

I didn't have another drink for a while, well, until Saturday when it was just a few and a couple of bets on the horses, but no luck. So I was back in the house for around ten or so where Annie was waiting in her usual spot on the settee watching some crap on TV.

"Well, how was your day, love?" I asked.

"Not too bad, just getting tired so easy now and could sleep the clock round," she replied with a yawn.

"Would you like a brew?"

"Yeah, why not?"

I went into the scullery and put the tea pot on then went into the bread bin and lifted out two slices of pan bread and stuck them under the toaster. When they were ready I put the butter on thick and poured the tea that was nice and strong. As we sat side by side on the settee eating our buttery toast and washing it down with the tea and with the warmth of the open fire, it was just perfect. Our wee house was a home and Annie made it feel that way.

The news came on the TV and it was a local bulletin.

"A body has been found in the lower Shankill and it is believed to be the work of the notorious Shankill Butchers. Police are looking any information and the whereabouts of a black taxi that was seen in the area around 9pm tonight. If you have any information you are to contact Tennent Street police station."

I sat there, in shock. "Oh my god, Annie, that's another one."

"Jimmy, this is terrible, nobody is safe. I don't like you staying out too late. Promise me you won't go to the bar at night. I don't mind you having a few beers but would rather you're home before it gets dark."

"Stop panicking, love. They are killing Catholics so I think I'm safe enough."

"You don't understand. Yeah, the Butchers are killing Catholics but the I.R.A. will retaliate and nobody knows with them. I wouldn't put it past them to blow up one of the bars again on the road or just riddle it with bullets. Nobody is safe anymore and I don't want our son growing up without a dad."

"Awk, Annie, wise up, it won't come to that."

"You don't know that, Jimmy. You haven't lived through the troubles here. The I.R.A. are ruthless and will do anything for a body count. They are tearing this country apart and the U.V.F. is just as bad, especially the Butchers. They show no mercy and if it's them who has done this murder then the I.R.A. will retaliate and I don't want you getting caught up in it."

"I won't, love," I replied, trying not to say too much. If only Annie knew that I personally knew the gang and knew they were to do a hit tonight. That's why I came home early. As they were coming back to the bar for a debrief, Daza wanted me there, but I made the excuse that Annie wasn't too well and I was worried about her. He didn't take it well but understood my reasons for not staying.

We finished our supper and went to bed. I didn't sleep too well as I was worried about a meeting I was to attend the next afternoon about the killing and it was the feeling within the U.V.F. that they were to stop these murders.

It was set for 3pm in a usual meeting place and it didn't go too well. Two of the gang attended along with myself and four other members of the U.V.F., one of whom was a guy called Billy, who was very vocal on his beliefs that the U.V.F. had to fight this war politically and not with the gun. I listened intently and to be honest he really did know what he was talking about, that we were so far behind the Sinn Féin that we were losing the political battle.

It finished with Sam and Billy falling out and idle threats were made, and it was when Daza spoke up and got it sorted that I thought it was going to come to blows. I was never so glad just to get out of there and to the bar for a couple of beers, just to get Billy and Daza to calm down and not start an internal feud within the team.

I had a chance to speak with Billy and everything he said was true, from the murders to the retaliation from the I.R.A., it was just a vicious circle that wouldn't end until we stepped out of the shadow and fought back through words and structured meetings with the politicians, the P.U.P. which was the political wing of the U.V.F., and he felt this was the way forward.

Annie, along with Billy, was right. The I.R.A. did strike back and it was in the form of a bomb on the Belfast-to-Dublin train where an innocent woman lost her life and two others were seriously injured.

This infuriated the U.V.F. and their campaign was stepped up.

The next few months, my time was taken up with a lot of meetings and arguments within the U.V.F. but it always got sorted and I got to understand the thinking and actions of certain people and their reasons for certain actions. I didn't agree with a lot of it but I knew when to keep my mouth shut and it was Billy that I got to know really well, and we became good friends as it was his ideology that I understood better than some of the other reactions which ended with the loss of life.

The weeks flew by and it was on the 14th of August that our wee baby made his appearance.

Annie was up all night with labour pains.

"Are you OK, love? Do you need anything?" I asked as another contraction came.

"I think it's time to go to hospital. Will you run round to my mum's and get her for me?"

"Yes, love. I will go straight away."

I took to my heels and went to get Lilly who got herself in a flop when I told her that Annie was in labour.

One of the neighbours did the needful and ran us down to the Mater hospital where Annie was admitted immediately and we were told to wait in reception until they did a few checks. After what felt like a lifetime I was brought into the delivery suite where Annie was in the middle of giving birth to our son.

"Are you OK, love?" I asked as I held her hand.

"Oh, Jimmy, it's sore," she said as a contraction came and she squeezed my hand. My heart went out to her; she really was in pain.

"It will be over soon. You're doing really well." I was useless. I couldn't do anything for her but just be there.

The machine that Annie was hooked up to started beeping and flashing and it was then the doctor said to me, "You will have to step back, sir, we need some room."

"What's wrong, Doctor?" I asked.

"The baby's heart rate is dropping. We need to get it delivered."

I looked at Annie. She was in real distress; she started crying. I was ushered back by a nurse who was now one of five dealing with Annie who were all in a bit of a panic. I could only watch on as the doctor delivered our son and as he lifted him over to a bench, he didn't cry and he was a kind of blue colour. It was then I started panicking. "What's going on, Doctor, is he OK?"

"Stay back, Mr. Andrews, we need to clear his airways."

I stood there in shock as he worked on him. I didn't know what to do. It felt like forever as I watched on and prayed our son would breathe.

And then he cried and what a relief just to hear that wee voice. A tear travelled down my cheek but I wiped it away before anyone saw.

"Mr. Andrews, can you see to your wife?" a nurse asked.

I lifted my head and could see Annie was distressed and crying. I rushed over and held her hand; she was freezing, really cold and shaking uncontrollably.

"Nurse, Nurse," I said worriedly.

The nurse came over immediately. "Doctor, come quick," she said quite loudly.

I knew there was something wrong. I looked around as my son was passed to one of the nurses and the doctor rushed over. He quickly examined Annie and called for a surgeon. "She is losing blood. Can someone get a surgeon? And quick."

I looked at the bed sheets which were now soaked in Annie's blood and it was the look on her face – I knew I was losing her. I went over and held her hand. "Annie, can you hear me? Don't leave me, don't go, please, please don't die." She opened her eyes and through the tears she smiled and then closed her eyes again.

I was ushered out of the room and back into the hall where another doctor rushed past me and went inside. I stood there, numb, not knowing what was going on.

Fifteen or twenty minutes had passed and the door opened. The two doctors came out. I stood with my mouth wide open, waiting and praying it was good news.

"Mr. Andrews, your wife is stable. She has lost a lot of blood but she is fine. You can come in and see her."

I was relieved at hearing that and all I could say was, "Thank you, Doctor, thank you."

I rushed past them to see Annie in bed, sleeping and hooked up to a machine. The nurse assured me she was fine and just needed rest.

"Where is our son?" I asked as I held Annie's hand which was a bit warmer than before.

"He is here." I looked up as another nurse had our son wrapped up in a blanket. She walked towards me and handed him to me. I felt so awkward taking him but the nurse assured me that he was fine and asked me to sit down and just nurse him.

As I looked at this wee bundle of joy; he was beautiful, just so perfect in every way. His blue eyes were piercing and his blond tufts of hair were so cute. It was the most perfect moment I had ever experienced. I could do nothing but stare at him.

"I will give him a bottle, Mr. Andrews, if that's OK. I'm sure he is hungry after that ordeal."

"Yes, I'm sure he is."

As the nurse took him off me she asked, "Have yous any names picked out for him?"

"Yeah, we do, he is going to be called Jonny," I said proudly.

"Awk, sure isn't that lovely? That really suits him," the nurse replied.

As she fed him a bottle I couldn't take my eyes off him. He was a wee gorb and had a good appetite.

"We will have to make an appointment with the orthopaedist for his wee foot."

"Why? What's wrong with his foot?" I asked.

"Sorry, Mr. Andrews, I thought the doctor told you."

"No, he didn't," I repeated. "What's wrong?"

The nurse lifted back the blanket to reveal Jonny's left foot which was twisted and bent up the wrong way. "Oh my god, what's wrong with it?" I said worriedly.

"It's just the way he grew in the womb but we will get it sorted."

"Will he be able to walk?"

"Of course he will. Stop worrying. We will get him back in a couple of weeks to see the specialist and get him sorted."

She wrapped him back up and handed him to me.

"Jimmy, what's wrong with him?"

I looked up and Annie was awake. I walked over with Jonny in my arms.

"Nothing that can't be fixed so don't be worrying, love, he's just perfect."

She outstretched her hands and I gave him to her. She was as overwhelmed as I was and just held him close to her chest and kissed his head.

"Are you OK, love? Do you feel OK?"

"Just tired but I'm OK now we have this wee one." She kissed him on the head again.

"I will go and let your mum know that everything is OK."

"Yes Jimmy, she will be up to high doe."

I left and went and gave the good news, which Lilly was chuffed to bits with. She was able to go and see them for five minutes which calmed her down and then we were asked to leave as they both needed to rest.

Over the next few days Annie and Jonny were kept in and I was able to feed him a few times and let her sleep. In fact she didn't get out for a solid week and then we had an appointment to see the specialist about Jonny's foot and get a plan put in place to get it fixed. The medical term for his condition was called talipes but it is normally called a club foot, where the foot is turned in and under.

He was put in Plaster of Paris every week for three months and every time it was changed his foot was moved back to, eventually, its proper position and then for the next two years he had to wear wee boots with a bar attached between them to keep his foot correct.

They were hard times, especially at night now that he was a toddler and didn't want to wear them, but after two years his foot was fixed and he was running about like a normal two-year-old.

*

Jonny was the one and only child Jimmy and Annie would have as there were complications with the birth and Annie had a blood clotting problem, and if another birth went wrong she could lose her life. So they both decided shortly after the birth of their son that they wouldn't have any more.

CHAPTER 22

THE SMELL OF SMOKE

The walks on a Sunday morning to Woodvale Park were a highlight of Annie's week as Jimmy got more and more involved, unbeknown to Annie, with the U.V.F. and his week was taken up with what she thought was a private loan company. She would not see much of him on a Saturday when he stayed most of the day and evening in the bar and a few nights a week at meetings.

It was after breakfast when they went for a walk up the road and into the park. The sun was high in the sky and with it being mid-August it was nice and warm.

"You were late home last night. What kept you?" Annie's tone was stern.

"Awk, you know how it goes, Annie, when you get into company."

"No, Jimmy, I don't. When you say you will be home for ten I expect you home."

"I know, love. I'm sorry, it won't happen again."

"Heard it all before, Jimmy." Annie walked a bit faster as she was annoyed with me.

I stopped and lit another cigarette and then caught up with her just as she got to our bench.

"Look, love, I'm just really busy at the minute with work and need a few beers on a Saturday just to relax."

"So when do you make time for us then?" she asked as she lifted Jonny out of his buggy.

"I'm here now and I will say to Daza about getting a day off during the week."

Jonny tugged at my trousers. I looked down. "What is it, son?" I said as I bent down.

"Ball, Daddy," he said. He loved kicking a football and to be honest I loved this time with him as it let me forget about all the other things going on in the week.

"Yes, son, let's kick the ball." I reached into the bottom of his buggy and lifted out his football. He might only be nearly three but he surely could kick a ball. We spent about a good hour or so kicking it back and forth and when I got him to take a penalty against me using two trees as nets, I would let him score and he just loved shouting, "Goal!" when he did.

It was the usual routine on a Sunday; park in the morning then lunch round at Annie's mum's which I wasn't fussed on, as on occasion I was on the receiving end of Lilly's sharp tongue and it got to the stage after one occasion that she took a swing at me with a poker when I answered her back, which I never did again.

I got the next few Wednesdays off and spent a bit more time with the family which pacified Annie a bit but then slowly and surely I slipped into my old ways and even managed to get out of going to her ma's on a Sunday, which gave me the opportunity for a few beers over in the club and I think Annie gave up moaning at me. So most of the time she didn't even mention it. As long as I weighed in around six and not too drunk she was happy enough.

Life on the Shankill at times was really hard and it was when the hunger strikes happened in 1981, when ten republicans died after starving themselves to death, that Sinn Féin became a prominent political party and spokesbody for the I.R.A.

But it was the I.R.A. that upped their campaign and over 7 months during the hunger strike they murdered 61 people.

13 policemen.

13 soldiers including 5 members of the Ulster Defense Regiment; the other 34 were civilians.

This infuriated the commanders of the U.V.F. who vowed revenge and it was then, one night in September, I was introduced to a man called Neil. He looked quite normal, not like a few other men I had met who were very frightening when they got heated about certain activities that they felt needed dealt with. Neil was around 5ft 9, slim built and not threatening-looking at all, in fact he just looked like a family man and even when he spoke he was quite reserved and softly spoken.

There was a hit organised for a known member of the I.N.L.A., which was another republican terrorist group. It was to take place on Friday night. The details were all in place and Neil was to do it. He obviously was quite nervous but was determined he could do it. He was to drive to the target's house and wait under the cover of darkness in his front yard for the target to come home, but he never did. Frustrated, he drove to the markets (a known republican area) to the target's girlfriend's house, but again, nobody home. Neil was now annoyed so in his wisdom he drove up the Ormeau road and he thought, with being in a known republican area, he shot dead the first man he came across.

Neil became someone I stayed away from but he rose through the ranks of the U.V.F. very quickly, known for his ruthlessness and talent for not just murder, but he brought a big income into the U.V.F. with bank robberies and hijackings.

It was when Neil got arrested and taken to Castlereagh holding centre that Daza was worried he would crack and give information up about the team, but he never did. Even though he was a mess when he was released and needed hospital treatment for a fractured jaw and cracked ribs, he never told the R.U.C. anything.

Billy was still banging on about distancing ourselves from criminality and trying to get things done politically but he was fighting a lost cause as the more the I.R.A. murdered, the call was for an eye for an eye and that's how it went.

The meetings went on for hours and at times I missed my 10 o'clock curfew that Annie had asked for, so usually when I came home drunk and stinking of cigarette smoke she was already in bed and when I saw a blanket on the settee I knew that was my place to sleep. It was one of these nights that she had had enough and stayed at her mum's that finished us.

It was a Friday night and I left the club around 12, slightly drunk as usual. It didn't take me long to walk home. I knew Annie was round at her mum's as we'd had a row earlier in the day and she told me she needed a break for a couple of days. I think she was trying to control me and my drinking but she was fighting a lost cause as between the painkillers and drink it was the only way I could get a night's sleep.

As I put the key in the door to go in, the house was in darkness. I pushed the door closed behind me and staggered up the stairs to go to the toilet. As I hadn't had much to eat that day I was famished and decided to make some chips. I put the chip pan on and peeled some spuds. As I waited for the fat to melt I went in and put the TV on and threw some coal on the fire. A knock came to the door. I thought Annie had forgotten her key. "Hold on, love. I'm coming now."

I staggered to the front door and opened it.

A figure stood there with his head down. I tried to focus on him but it was dark.

"Can I help you? Are you lost?"

He lifted his head. I gasped at who it was. "You!" I said in surprise.

"Hi, Craig. Remember me?"

As I stood there staring at him I didn't know what to say. This old man stood in front of me with his scarred face and just as I went to answer he made a grab for me. Grabbing me by the throat, two handed, he pushed me backwards into the living room and onto the settee we fell. His grip loosened and I broke free. "Joe, what the fuck are you doing?" I slurred.

He grabbed me again but this time was on top of me, squeezing my throat.

"You, you killed my Mary and did this to me, now it's time to die."

I tried and tried to break free but it was useless. He

was extremely strong and in vain I fought back but lost this fight and my life along with it.

After Joe murdered me he stood over my body lying on the settee, laughing. "I got you, you wee fucker. I got you."

He fixed anything that had been knocked over and then noticed the now boiling fat in the pan on the cooker and that's when he decided to make it look like an accident and lit the oil and after closing the door behind him, he smiled and left into the darkness.

It was soon after the house was engulfed with smoke and a neighbour alerted the fire service that Jonny arrived home with Billy, who was now his boss and manager of Heather Street social club. I would never know how Jonny turned out and if Annie ever found happiness but my life had ended with Joe having the last say and I only could have regrets for the time I lived on the Shankill road and with Annie.

Craig James Andrews or formally known as Jason Stephens, born August 16th 1954 to Nigel and Dorothy and along with his sister Paula, didn't ever find out who his real parents were. He died 18th November 1994 at the hands of child abductor and abuser Joe Garrett, whereabouts unknown, at age 40. Jimmy's life was full of dark tragic moments but it was when he lived on the Shankill and met Annie his past life became a distant memory and for once in his life he was accepted and for the short period was happy. Even during his time in the U.V.F. he was admired and was given a send-off with full colours and will always be remembered as our Jimmy.

By the same author also available on Amazon
THE LIFE OF JONNY ANDREWS SERIES:

JONNY THE BOY FROM THE ROAD (BOOK 1)
PAYBACK JONNY'S REVENGE (BOOK 2)
LIFE'S A BEACH OR A NIGHTMARE (BOOK 3)
FRACTURED (BOOK 4)

ABOUT THE AUTHOR

My love for writing has gripped me, I have found a new passion.

My four sons inspires me every time I hear what is going on in their lives and feel I can only get better as time goes by.

Printed in Great Britain
by Amazon

65877434R00108